Wish You Were Here

Wish You Were Here

Eliza Tudor

Minerva Rising • Atlanta
2017

© 2017 by Eliza Tudor

Published by
Minerva Rising Press
6025 Tangletree Dr
Roswell, GA 30075-6013

ISBN: 978-0-9990254-4-4

www.minervarising.com

All rights reserved. Other than excerpts for review or commentaries, no part of this book may be reproduced without permission of the copyright holder.

For Lance, Cleo, and Dexter. Always.

Contents

zero	1
one	2
two	8
three	24
four	33
five	40
six	53
seven	72
eight	90
nine	102
ten	109
eleven	115
epilogue	118
Acknowledgments	120

zero

You are here. You were there. You are here now. You need to get over there. And it all comes down to time.

Freddie tried to see it in her mind. Paper was certainly simpler; reality was different. Eyes open, her fingers sliding across metal, her head vibrating against a rack, Freddie knew she had to move. Everything was louder, bigger, colder, brighter than even she'd imagined. She had less than a minute. If they caught her now they'd find the map and the USB drives in her pocket.

Her server was only an aisle away. Nose running, her ears packed; the sound was overwhelming. *Wear your headphones.* Freddie had trouble hearing on a good day—*too much listening?*—let alone in the main aisle of a data center the size of six football fields. A data center filled beyond capacity with room after room of whirring servers, the fans even louder. Racks refrigerated to keep all the machinery, that vast land of information, cold.

Why did I even come here?

Freddie could see her server. The yellow cords almost in reach. The only one with a keyboard. *Don't think. Don't remember.* It was now or never. *But I want to remember everything.*

She began to count backwards. Ten. Nine. Eight. It was almost time. She knew what would happen if she stepped out too early. If they caught her. Four. Three. Two.

one

You are here. It's what all the signs said. Posted between office buildings and parking lots, beside the battalions of bikes that were multicolored on one side of the street and white on the other. This Silicon Valley was as real as it was metaphorical, a place between, a valley enclosed by decidedly different mountains. One set reddish, shaped like the bare toes of a giant. The other set misty on mornings like this one, hazy green, with roads twisting beneath the boughs of redwoods. Some kind of middle.

Update status. You are here now. Welcome to Middlefield.

Middlefield, one of several Silicon Valley city-states inhabited by the workers of tech. Pledge allegiance and don't be evil! Look right or left at street level: the neighborhoods, the forsaken office parks, the fully branded corporate campuses. Alive or abandoned.

This is what it will be like at the end of the world, Freddie thought as she ran her usual early morning path between empty campuses. The roses that once lined the sidewalk of the abandoned Superfund site were so overgrown they were almost dangerous. But Freddie, her mind spinning towards dystopia, felt good as a mid nineties/early-aught pop mix began to play. Her bracelet—tracking GPS, blood pressure, heart rate, steps per minute, music—matched automatically to motion. Cloud in control because *tell me what you want, what you really, really want.*

They startled Freddie, coming up so fast from behind. It was the squat Asian woman (who *had* to be the same age as Freddie) and her impossibly young, model-shaped, also Asian girlfriend. As the couple bounded up, with their two blue-eyed huskies, a sound emerged from a surprised Freddie—a frightened grunt, something between *hi* and *oh*. There was no mistaking it; Freddie jumped. Her left earbud even fell out. They'd scared her, but still, never a good thing to start the week shouting, "Ho!" to your May–September lesbian neighbors.

Freddie was usually here alone, running between the empty buildings. The humans waved an apology as Freddie watched their progress. Still slightly shamed into a trot, Freddie noted their particular variety of legs in motion, trying to return to her kind of pace.

Begin Scene. The dogs tore through the ivy. The sound they made crisp and cutting. She heard them behind her, their stride swift, almost at her feet. She jumped higher, over dumpsters. They were coming for her. Now, she thought. Over that fence. Run harder. Now! End scene.

Pretending was always easier for Freddie. In reality, she'd done nothing but trot on buckled sidewalk. Freddie attempted a low barrier with caution. The parking lot would be empty for another hour; the sky effortlessly blue, running shorts year-round. Oh, this Californ-IA. Freddie, afraid of unleashed dogs, most strangers, bad drivers, and—always—germs, disliked running but did it anyway. It got her out of the house. It was virtuous. She would bring her children back later to ride bikes, the youngest setting up orange cones in the abandoned parking lot. Eight more blocks to go; Freddie panting.

I saw the sign and it opened up my mind.

Freddie's family and her neighbors in Middlefield lived in identical slender townhomes between an electric train track and a maze of alleyways. They peered into each other's rooms and garages, knowing the shows their neighbors watched and the instruments their children were made to practice. They knew their neighbors' discipline methods, the habits of their pets, and all the items purchased in bulk. They knew the hobbies their neighbors abandoned or were about to begin, passions often stored between the vehicle they took to be washed and the recycling bins. But their proximity—their intimacy—was only verified after a few glasses of wine at children's parties. Where they blushed and stammered, "Saw you got a new fixie," meaning: *You must have vested and bought yourself a fixed-gear titanium Lynskey to ride to work*. The customs of the county: a privileged ghetto, a neighborhood surrounded entirely by work. For some people.

"You are now crossing Middlefield," the crosswalk intoned for the visually impaired. This included not only the blind but also those staring at screens. It also included the daydreamers of this world, like Freddie. Freddie traversed all four lanes deep in her own narration.

Turn left, but mind the gap; the haves and the have-nots were neighbors. This land neither your land nor my land. That was the real story of Silicon Valley. Nobody *real* was making it. The few shacks and rusted motor homes, perhaps still around from the old days when the entire valley was an orchard, now sat between the maze of townhomes and corporate campuses. This land that once held stone fruit trees all in a row, cherries and peaches at attention towards the mountains, now housed people living in rusted-out campers and shacks with no heating (tiny backyard) *and* those in $7,000/month townhomes and garages with Lynskeys and Lotuses (no backyard).

The shack with the *No Turn U: private property* sign was Freddie's favorite. Freddie enjoyed their lemon trees and fake geraniums, their burnt grill and ladder always open. It was an intoxicating mix. Real people who sat outside and seemed to be in no hurry! Freddie tried to look through the windows every time she passed. The police caution tape still up. The shack probably worth a million-five, easy, because of the land. Who owned the land? That was the question. God Bless America.

The train station finally in sight, Freddie began to slow her pace. She watched Jaya-Next-Door's nanny, Miss Manvinder, arriving for the day. Jaya called her by a different name, her "house" name, *Meer-a*. Indians had Indian nannies, the Chinese and Koreans had grandparents, and the former Soviets had young babushkas or Eastern bloc babysitters with tight, crystal-encrusted, stonewashed jeans. Everyone either American-born, H-1B'd, or green carded to the fullest extent of the law. Third Culture ruled.

Freddie walked the last block, her breath and the breeze cooling her. Early morning in Middlefield always smelt of flowers and sea salt. *Don't step on the snails!* Only brown people outside, she noticed, resisting the urge to power fist and waving instead. "Why does everything have to be political or mean something?" her husband always asked her. "The personal *is* the political," she'd murmur, knowing the reference was entirely lost on him. Still, Freddie was glad that those doing *actual work* were gifted the best time of day. Freddie smiled at the Latino landscapers with their long sleeves, the Latina cleaners and nannies heading to vacuum IKEA rugs and watch blonde children at perfect playgrounds (only parents took them to campus parking lots). The people with grandparents in Iowa or Pennsylvania—and the blonde Brazilians—had a Maria. The Germans and the English just went to daycare. The French trusted no one.

I could be a spy, Freddie thought. *I should have been a spy.* "That time I tried to join the FBI" filed itself under possible cocktail story options. Like Freddie ever went out for cocktails now.

She looked over at the The Hub. 10 API—a public school harder to get into than Stanford. Sponsored by The Company, her husband's employer, it was education at its finest. Freddie hadn't even gotten on the waiting list to the waiting list of the The Hub lottery, but *if* The Hub *were* their school she could just walk across the street. Freddie shouldn't complain; they only walked two short hills to their 5 API school, and the kids complained enough to last both hills.

"Battery low," came the shitty-voiced reminder in her ear. The Gin Blossoms greatest hit petering off to nothingness. The music was gone. Freddie began to hear birds and feel the Priuses passing her, her earbuds still in. She needed to get home. Mister needed to get out the door. People to wake, breakfast to make, showers to take. Time to hurry. *Fake, bake, cake, quake. Enough!* The last sign for yet another Omni-ynga-cell-tech-indra across from the neighborhood gate: Lobby, blue dot. You are here, red dot. Freddie flipped to shuffle. It worked for only a moment. *It's the end of the world as we know it and I feel*

Fine.

"Beautiful day," Freddie called out to Miss Manvinder.

Freddie was running late. The man with Pebbles the Pekingese stopped in the wet grass instead of the sidewalk just so he wouldn't have to speak. Freddie saw him and understood. The man nodded as Freddie hurried past. She always said hello to Pebbles and the man. If only she could remember his name.

Freddie Flint-Smythe kept her name. Of course she did. A hyphenate at birth, vintage Seventies. A character born—named for the great aviatrix, explorer, cartographer, and yet-another-who-never-grew-elderly, the writer/adventurer: Fredericka "Freddie" von Duran Hatton-Heath, whose famous books *Above the Serengeti* and *Beyond the End of the World* were read, to great influence, by the Reverend Thaddeus E. D. Flint-Smythe (father of Freddie) while Freddie was still in her mother's womb.

There were few hyphenates in the center of Indiana in the mid-Seventies and Eighties—in the Nineties, for that matter. Heck, swing by today, to the corner of Oak and Ford or Main and Pine, and you'd struggle to find a hyphenate, certainly of the sub-four footer crowd. *Why do you have that line in your name?* If Freddie had a quarter for every time she'd heard that one.

"My parents were . . . are . . ." Hippies? Perhaps delve deeper, to the heart of the matter, to the heart of the matter of the mother of all Mothers, one Joan Flint-Smythe. Yes, there you go. Knew you'd go there. Don't we all? Yes, don't we all. A little aristo-gloss in the cornfields? Smell it. Under the sweat and motor oil. Under the manure. But aren't we better for it?

Just one of the stories told too many times.

In the beginning. It was all biblical really, meaning, the story of families. Rev. Thad and Joan Flint-Smythe's brood—there were five of them born. Freddie was the only girl, thanks to the vinegar. An old wives' tale, acid for a girl. All wanted. All a mother's masterpiece. All a father's prayer. All in the middle of Indiana, near the middle of America. Freddie *was* the middle. You see, there was a fire. The parsonage burned, children lost. There was a Before family and an After family. Freddie, once the youngest child, became—for a few years—the only. And then, she was the eldest— all that remained from the previous childhood.

See Freddie take beets for lunch instead of baloney. See Freddie homesick from school often. See Freddie take six showers a day but save the water for the ducks and the asparagus bed. See Freddie then.

But you are *here*. See Freddie now. See Freddie in Silicon Valley, wife and mother, heading rapidly to midlife, two children (two miscarriages), no pets (blame the housing market), oh Cali-Mama. See Freddie, the Superheroine (but more on that to come).

TL;DR: It is the end of the world and Freddie wrote a memoir. She likes spy movies and detective novels. She supports PBS. She works parttime for The Outsourcers, but don't tell the neighbors or their nannies or the other moms at drop-off/pick-up. Non-Compete/Non-Disclosure! She buys flowers for others. She buys plants for herself.

Freddie Flint-Smythe opened the door of their rented townhouse at 6:52 a.m. and kicked off her neon running shoes. *I'm home!*

You are here.

two

"We need you to write a memoir." That's how it began last year. Rosemary Rafferty said it before Freddie even got comfortable. Rosemary's office looked like something out of a romance novel. Plush, overblown, tufted everything. It was in stark contrast to The Outsourcers' lobby, which was minimalist acacia.

"You're our best candidate for this." Rosemary smiled. "No modesty, Freddie, you make tech guys sexy. Online. We have an untapped market that we need to tap, tap, tap in a big way. Boomers, our dear TechMamas, our HipsterDudes, everyone wants a memoir. You already know the entire Apple campus *thinks* they're writers. We need you to branch out."

Freddie's job for The Outsourcers went something like this: Ghostwriter/Emergency Preparedness Specialist/Gestational Doula (hours limited until her youngest went Kinder)/Burner Re-entry. But the ghostwriting was her primary focus for The Outsourcers. Freddie Flint-Smythe wrote the majority of the holiday letters sent in Silicon Valley. Her thank you notes were becoming a status symbol. For the most part, Freddie wrote social media posts, but sometimes Cyrano-level work was involved. Okay, modesty aside. Online romance profiling was a specialty.

Her client roster was fairly divided. Often single Indian/Korean/forty-two-year-olds-from-Nebraska tech guys or Mormon/formerly-Midwestern TechMamas. Neither group had the time or energy to keep up with the level of literary output their social lives demanded. That was

Freddie's job.

The Valley TechMama needed to keep the mother-in-law in Salt Lake happy and the sisters-in-law everywhere jealous. A basement full of the most up-to-date survival gear and the best family disaster plan money could buy wasn't hardly enough. Freddie and The Outsourcers' chef, Carl, taught the Mama's children everything their own mothers and grandmothers taught them—gardening, pickling, baking, and canning—while providing beautifully lit shots of the proceedings (employees' arms and legs Photoshopped out and Mama's placed in). All with updates to their family blog (which Freddie maintained).

"I don't know how Amy does it! Her Google job, three kids, a size-two triathlete, and now, her own pickles! How?" Simple. She outsources. Amy has a Freddie.

The guys, well, Freddie just made them interesting and communicative. Good listeners, empathetic. Someone you could have fun with, for a lifetime. Ryan Gosling meets Kevin Rose (or even a Young Bre Petis). Any ethnicity would do as long as they seemed destined for the cover of *Wired*. Now add climbing crampons, artisan vodka, and a banjo. Basically Bay Area date bait. At least, on screen. It was Belinda's job to prep them for actual facetime—Belinda, The Outsourcers' Manners/Charm Expert.

But a memoir?

"Think of it as an extended Christmas letter." Rosemary used her reassuring voice, the one she usually saved for clients. "Our people want memoirs."

"But—"

Rosemary stopped Freddie with a well-manicured hand, the collection of gold and leather bangles falling up her pearly arm.

"Our clients want to share the moment in their lives that shaped them, the time that created the person they've become. Okay. We know how much they love credentials and you have that MFA. Let's put it to some use." Rosemary barely paused. "And you have a story. We both know it. Write it! I'll make sure it gets published. We can ask double your current rate."

Rosemary finally took a breath. She looked like she might say ohm. Namaste even. What else was there to talk about? Both of them knew Freddie wouldn't say no. Double her current rate? *Hello?* Freddie was hooked.

Rosemary turned to face her screen. "Didn't you do that NaNoWriMo thing for several clients in November? That was in a month, wasn't it?"

"Rosemary, I can't write a memoir in a month." Freddie knew it was impossible even if she did have at least four different drafts of something akin to a memoir already on her backup drive.

"Freddie." Rosemary's face seemed to blossom. That smile, those eyes. That flick of patrician pale hair, all golds and silvers. Rosemary pulled her greige cashmere shawl around her and snuggled deeper into her seat. "My dear, you can do anything. That's why I call you our Superheroine."

Rosemary pushed a piece of notepaper across her desk, nails like five beautiful sharks. Freddie had always wanted written numbers pushed in her direction. A dream come true. Rosalind Russell was playing Freddie in the film version even as she waited to turn the paper over. "I'll triple that amount if you get it done by the end of the month."

It wasn't Google stock. It wasn't like a big IPO. It wasn't like a small IPO. It was nothing compared to what Silicon Valley even calls a bonus. But to Freddie, and nearly everyone else on the planet, it was more zeros than she'd ever held at one time. A comma was involved. Even if it was nothing but numbers on notepaper yet, Freddie couldn't help it; she multiplied immediately. *Closer to the goal.*

"The end of the calendar month or thirty days from now?" Freddie swallowed hard, already thinking of the boxes she would need to pull from the storage unit under their townhouse. *Those* boxes. And she'd have to wade through her backup file.

Rosemary barely turned from her screen. "My dear, what is time? Go ahead and make it thirty-one."

Thirty-one days hath the month of Remember.

It started long before that month. There were all those tries on Freddie's backup to prove it (time-stamped if you're interested). And Freddie would certainly be lying if she said the idea of a book—a physical object on a shelf with pages and a cover and her name on it—wasn't her life's dream. Rosemary knew exactly what buttons to push and those to leave for Freddie to press, repeatedly, herself. But before she even left Rosemary's office, Freddie was asking herself: *How can I pull this off without feeling completely smarmy? The* story. *Her* version. That moment in her own life that was a time of before and after—at least, the one she was willing to tell.

"This is the right woman for the job. She taught Emily Dickinson to terrorists. She can handle our clients." It was the way Rosemary Rafferty had introduced Freddie to the Round Table, what everyone at The Outsourcers called the lunchroom.

"Terrorists, really?" Even Soo-Jin (The Outsourcers' Professional Tiger Mom-For-Hire) looked a little impressed.

Not again.

I have told this story too many times, Freddie thought. She'd told it after being shipped back to Indiana. She'd told it at cocktail parties and on first dates. She'd told it in a formal university lobby to students interested in Central Asia. She'd even told a heavily edited version to groups of Christian women in living rooms and banquet halls. It was the look on the women's faces that Freddie remembered, a mix of envy and unrequited passion. The women didn't love *her*. They loved how she made them feel. For just over a half an hour, Freddie gave them the chance to join the Peace Corps and fly to a place they'd never heard of, full of lost boys and girls in golden scarves and maps. And then, be evacuated with fifteen minutes notice by the United States Marines.

Freddie was enough like them—small town, Indiana—enough like their daughters or granddaughters, but just that bit different. They could've been her! A female James Bond meets Indiana Jones (albeit Smythe) from Indiana. One of their own. Or, at least, that's how Freddie sold it.

They couldn't get enough of her in the Heartland, after The Talk. What her parents (or maybe it was just Joan) dubbed her "Lecture Series." Have a little pity. They were fraught years, and Freddie, always sensitive, was still processing. Plus, she needed the money.

"Never again," Freddie said finally. "I can't explain Islam and yurts to any more women in pink blazers. All that Cool Whip! All those folding chairs! Enough!" As if that was the real problem. Her father nodded. Her mother shrugged. The slides, the handicrafts, the boxes of journals and letters, the printed-out emails, the photocopied and hand-drawn maps were put where they belonged—in storage.

Until now.

Freddie could say it was Rosemary; it was work. But the first timestamp on her backup drive coincided with their first day in California, before Freddie ever knew The Outsourcers existed. Mister in his new cool job at The Company ("the best place to work on the planet") building Clouds (that place where all information goes to live). Her job: two small children.

"Working from home," that's what people in TechLand called it. A euphemism. Very few in the Valley did it longer than the length of m/paternity leave. Maybe a day or two during flu season, but come on. Haven't you listened to Sheryl? The whole idea of staying at home was antiquated, so last century. "Remind me," the parents asked Freddie at the sand park on Saturdays, "what do you do?"

"I'm a writer," Freddie explained. Sure. Write. Right. She typed during naptimes. It was the sheer volume in her backup drive that disturbed her. All those drafts filed away in her computer waiting for yet another draft.

And there was the day Mister came home from work and, whilst pouring himself a cold Belgian, began to tell her about the interesting book he'd just heard reviewed on NPR during his ride home. "You are going to love it," he said. "It's everything you talk about."

"What's the title?" She was pulling condiments from the fridge, turning towards the stove just before the buzzer rang out.

"Female? Feminine-something."

No. It couldn't be. It wasn't. She barely stopped. Her finger on the timer, balancing catsup bottles and the makings of an excellent vinaigrette.

"You're not talking about *The Feminine Mystique* are you?" Her throat tightened. She heard him saying, "That's it! That's the book!" as if very far away.

It had to be fifty years old. Plus a few. She wanted to smack him. She wanted to smack herself. (*It's everything you talk about?*) She was probably still sucking her thumb the first time she'd read Betty Freidan and he was thinking she might—no. *No!* She was the product of feminism, a graduate of a women's college; Freddie stood straighter in front of the stove. Anarchist, punk even. Patti Smith did it, for goodness sake. This was art! This was a radical act, a kind of supreme performance, the giving of oneself, an act of devotion in service to others, years of life, decades for a purpose. She'd created something beyond a page or a stage, beyond a painting. Not just a character. Not just one. Two people! Actual humanity. Souls! Freddie built them and their specific, individualized yet integrated world, and he's bringing Betty Freidan home for dinner?

It's everything you talk about. There was something there, Freddie conceded, placing the catsup bottle. (Her mother, Joan, never would've put a bottle on the table. *Get a ramikan!*) What was a choice, a reality, a function, an economic—an artistic—decision? And what had merely happened? Who was conning whom?

After their first year in California, Freddie stopped talking about her writing at the playground. It was ridiculous; she was ridiculous. It was a naptime hobby, really. What Freddie did full-time was everything else. *Maybe someday* was the answer for everything. But then Rosemary happened. The Outsourcers happened. A part-time answer that took Freddie over, The Outsourcers was both relief and fulfillment. Freddie believed in coincidence. They'd met three times. The first time should have been enough.

The bike path/exercise trail ran directly beside the elementary school garden plots where Freddie, garden volunteer for Mrs. Vance's kindergarten class, had been working on a Sunday. Her kids were revelling in the weekend-empty school playground. Her husband was beside them, looking at his phone while Freddie, at a distance, hunched over Room Two's raised beds, thinning carrots. Freddie discovered The Outsourcers only because perfect almost-sixty-year-olds jog on Sunday mornings in Silicon Valley.

"Yours is the best," Rosemary said, panting a little.

"Thanks." Freddie was too tired to think up the better, more Nora Charles response of "Truthfully, I agree," which she thought of later, around 3:30 a.m. in bed.

Freddie didn't realize this was the woman who would change her life.

"Do you teach?" Rosemary asked, the tube of her camelpack to her lips. She took a sip. Freddie stood.

"Not anymore. Oh." It took Freddie more time than necessary in those days. "You were wondering about here? No, I'm not a teacher here.

I'm just a parent volunteer. I help the students learn about gardening. It's fun. We do tastings and sensory exercises and learn about preparing healthy food. Mostly snacks." The practiced tone now forming, the overly cheerful Mama. *I'm happy? You're happy? We're happy together?*

"You *were* a teacher." Rosemary didn't seem quite impatient, and her tone was factual. "What did you teach?"

Freddie was too tired for this. She wanted to get back to the carrots. *Stop talking, Freddie. Please.* Did she just repeat all of that? It was pitiful. Freddie went on and on about how she used to teach at a small college—literature and writing mostly—but now, sadly, adjunct work wouldn't cover a babysitter. Freddie was ridiculous, as if no one had ever asked her a question before. Later, around 3:40 a.m., Freddie wondered how lonely she might actually be.

"What hourly rate would you like?" Rosemary curved her back slightly into a kind of yoga move.

Oh great, Freddie thought. *Another one.* Hadn't she learned her lesson being nice to the checkout guy at the 7/11? Midwestern doesn't translate well in the South Bay.

Rosemary held out a card.

The Outsourcers
We accomplish what you don't have time for.
Rosemary Rafferty, Founder

"Call me at the office tomorrow and we'll set up an appointment. You're perfect for us."

And Rosemary started back up, jogging the trail. Her butt firmer than Freddie's would ever be. Rosemary turned her head one last time: "Call." But Freddie didn't. *Two small children!* Life happened and continued thus.

The Elementary School Holiday Festival was the occasion of their second meeting. Freddie's booth was perfection. She'd just thought, "What Would My Mother Do?" and Joan's voice sounded in her head: *Height, Shine, Aspiration, Attainment!*

The president of the PTA opened the doors, and Freddie, in her apron, was more than prepared—until Rosemary Rafferty walked through the side door of the school's multi-use-room and went straight to Freddie's booth, saying, "Hello again. I'll take it all." Months of work, only to sell everything in the very first minute? After all that setup? Well. Okay. And to Rosemary Rafferty, of all people, who wrote her check, saying, "You never called."

It was embarrassing. The explanation was worse. Freddie didn't have *time*? She'd braided and baked thirty loaves of gluten-free bread. She'd stayed up all night to make zippered bags. Two young children, her husband's odd Valley hours, everything sounded absurd in front of *this* booth, to *this* woman.

"Ten hours a week total," Rosemary said. "We could start with that. You could do most of it at home. Say only two hours a week out of the house, with the clients." She placed her check in Freddie's palm. "We pay extraordinarily well."

Of course, Freddie thought about calling. She planned the call. Rehearsed it over the long school holiday. But then, life intervened. Her boy—her youngest—needed the second surgery of his life. (At night, while they all slept, Freddie feared. You know how her older brothers died. Pray for the health of your boys and the safety of your girls—isn't that the prayer they taught her to pray?)

Grandmothers would call this issue of his a clubbed foot. It's better, more appropriate to say CTEV these days—*congenital talipes equinovarus*—or, simply, *talipes*. He was a handsome child, Freddie's boy, brown curls, hazelnut skin, and large gray eyes. He looked almost Edwardian in pictures, and though it seems an antique ailment, that twist in exactly the spot where it should never be was very real. Freddie could make a map of his feet. How Freddie worked that skin, those ankles, those muscles and bones.

This child of Freddie's, as often happens in life, was athletically inclined; nature giveth exactly what nature taketh away. All children in Middlefield had to excel at *something*, didn't they? It was required in the Peninsula, as if they were all being represented instead of parented. Freddie's eldest, a girl, had begun coding low-level apps in kindergarten. She also read early and washed her hands obsessively. Thank you, Mama and Daddy. Freddie's second, this boy—no Peyton Manning, but still. *Who taught that boy how to throw? His mother, that's who.* And the third? No. There was no third. There would be no third.

Period.

So Freddie was mother/nurse once again. Ponseti method, French functional method, splints, braces, massage therapy, yoga, tai chi, gymnastics, surgery (now *surgeries*), Freddie tried it all. A five-year-old and a recuperating two-year-old made Rosemary Rafferty disappear. Nearly. It would be dishonest not to admit that the rectangular business card and the memory of their earlier meetings were taken out and pondered at irregular intervals.

But then, First Freedom! A new school year, and as Freddie brewed the inaugural coffee of the day at 5:00 a.m. on that second Wednesday in September, when both children were finally healthy and headed back to school and the prospect of three completely free mornings a week bubbled forth, Freddie thought of Rosemary's card. She'd kept it, after all, in the drawer with the batteries and Band-Aids, just beneath the coffee maker. Freddie told herself she would call.

After drop-offs and her errands, in that halcyon two hours and forty-five minutes before the pick-ups began. *Really*, she would call! But Freddie didn't have to. As things sometimes happen in life as they often do in fiction, it was that very day in the Target paper towel aisle that Freddie met Rosemary Rafferty for the third time and sealed the deal.

Freddie didn't hide it quickly enough—her Emergency Preparedness List. The purchases she made every California September and stored in their townhome's lower level. Paper towels and trash bags were near the end of the list, so Freddie's cart already overflowed with medical supplies, storable food, batteries, and enormous bottles of water and bleach when Rosemary Rafferty stopped her in her tracks.

Blame the years of days and hours and minutes. Caring for small children (and never sleeping) make you open and raw. The waking at 5:00 a.m. for years to write a thousand hard words so she could still, secretly, think herself a writer didn't help. The loneliness inherent in both of her "jobs" was palpable. It wasn't just the list; Freddie couldn't hide quickly enough. Rosemary saw everything. Freddie might even have told her, between the stacked rolls of white, about how when the youngest napped Freddie would sometimes fall asleep on the couch only to wake minutes later. She'd felt it. The ground shook her awake. She would pitch to her side, grabbing her phone in one motion, the real-time earthquake map always open. The preparations forever ready. The lists, maps, essential belongings, packed backpacks, passports, cash, documents, everything accounted for: Health. Safety. Survival. Freddie had a plan. She would save them.

She didn't trust the government's seismographs, so Freddie would text her husband: *Did we jst hve a tremor?* Nope. It was only the train, the electric one that passed through their neighborhood. Or, perhaps, the Cal-Train only two blocks away. And still, Freddie didn't believe, didn't trust the data. The rumble beneath woke her. The ground shook. She was sure of it. She'd felt it. But the world had yet to end.

Freddie followed Rosemary's BMW carefully. *Thou shalt not tailgate.*

"My son would love your car," Freddie said, pushing shut the heavy door on her own dented Eighties Volvo wagon. Rosemary's car was red, shiny, luxuriously new. Freddie's youngest "collected" red cars as they drove. *Stop talking, Freddie.* Freddie followed Rosemary, entering the headquarters of The Outsourcers through the front door.

Located in an Eichler-designed strip mall between Sunnyvale and Cupertino, The Outsourcers had an impressive entry. At least for Silicon Valley. It wasn't the atrium that got the clientele, it was the wall of photographs: Rosemary sitting at a kitchen table with Mark and Priscilla. Drinking smoothies with Steve and Laurene. Seated on a couch alongside the family Brin. Sipping drinks on the Pages' lanai. Sheryl and Rosemary laughing in tree pose. The photo with Al Gore looked as if a press release might need to be issued (call TMZ). Ditto Woz. Various mayors, governors, senators, and starlets aside. Spot The Clintons. The Dalai Lama. George Lucas. Enough said.

Like most one-industry communities, a sheep mentality abides in the South Bay. If it's good enough for _____, it's good enough for me. Fill in that blank Silicon Valley-style—be it with a Brin, a Page, a Sandberg, or a Zuck—and you have a client base lined up like Chinese funeral statues, one after another, all waiting (some more patiently than others) to pay for the right to outsource the way Sergey does. The way Steve did.

They do it daily in their offices, why not in their homes? If the job took time, if it was difficult, if it was mind-numbingly simple, someone else could do it. Someone else *should* do it. But not just anyone. We need the people Steve trusted.

If The Outsourcers' wall of fame was gratuitous, the lobby décor minimalist, then the secretary could well be described as cartoonish. Willa was everything Rosemary was not. Rosemary may have posed for the pictures, but Willa was the voice that answered the call: "You have reached the office of The Outsourcers. Willa speaking. How may we be of service?"

"A good morning, Rosemary," Willa called as soon as the door opened. "And Freddie." Willa's voice *was* The Outsourcers, and a Dickensian plum of a voice it was. Reassuring, alternating posh and pikey, Willa was full busted, with large, owlish glasses, her hair cut in a severe aubergine-tinted bob, and at that moment, affecting a cheerfulness that the English can only possess after decades of California sunshine.

"You *must* be Freddie. No, my dear, no last names, please. Rule number one for Outsourcers' associates. Our founder, whom you've met several times it seems, is the only one with a last name in this realm." Willa trilled her *r* slightly for the audience. "Rosemary checked in on the drive and I have everything ready. We're pleased you've finally come in. I've put the kettle on. And here." She handed Freddie an embossed cover. "All information is considered helpful. Our most comfortable chair." Her arm outstretched, her eyes already back to her desk.

"See you in a moment," Rosemary called, shutting the door to what Freddie assumed was her sanctum. Now that Freddie was hooked, she belonged to Willa. To be left in the comfortable chair with a screen in her lap, to fill out "information" on virtual pages.

1. List every job you've ever had.

Every single one?

Willa didn't even look up from her desk, her voice shifting to something harder, something not quite Anglican. "Paid and unpaid. Doesn't need to be chronological. Dates don't matter as much as specificity. Be detailed. Take your time."

Okay.

The known quantities. Then, of course, the multitude of office jobs, the bouquet of courses and degrees with various levels of completion, and all those acting gigs. A little spice: *Elvis Impersonator, Drummer/Back-up vocals* (a short-lived, all-girl band that played county fairs and birthday parties in the early '90s—*The Jennifers*—Freddie had been the only non-Jen),

Software Beta Tester, and *Surveillance Technician specializing in photography and scenarios* . . . Freddie had yet to finish the sentence when Willa handed over a teacup and peeked.

"A fairly average resume for an Outsourcer contains fifty discrete jobs," Willa said over Freddie's shoulder, clocking *Surveillance* approvingly. "Discrete, as in -ete, separate and distinct."

"I'm sorry, I'm not quite done." Freddie flushed. "I haven't gotten to retail yet. Or the service industry." Or the really lousy jobs.

Willa leaned and stirred her own cup above Freddie. She sighed. "The corporate universe may be too daft to see it, but we, here at The Outsourcers, are great fans of The Interesting Generation. The overeducated and underemployed, smug, self-loathing coterie who came of age under the eyes of Mr. Rogers and Nancy Reagan. *Just Say No* and *It's you I like*. Three graduate degrees—at least. Multiple languages. Homemaking skills out the you-know-what—we especially adore the Midwesterners here. *Exactly* what Rosemary Rafferty wants." Willa took a sip. "People who can quilt, write a screenplay, teach a child—or adult—to read in at least four languages, pickle anything, bake for the allergic, garden, stake out a cheating spouse, birth a baby in a pinch, and put together a decent playlist. Accomplishing a few of these tasks at the same time. Yes, my dear, keep going."

Freddie was still considering the qualities inferred with the term *smug* when she sat down finally to face Rosemary Rafferty—the only person at The Outsourcers allowed two names—but Freddie shouldn't have worried. For the moment, for Rosemary Rafferty, Freddie was the right woman for the job(s). And she wasn't alone.

"Are you in a hurry? I'd like you to meet a few of your colleagues." This morning should have been sacrosanct, an extra 1,000 words at least after the errands. But on this day, Freddie barely glanced at the clock.

They were seated at a round table, eating a mix of meals. A breakfast sandwich in front of one, salads and rice in front of two others, and a bowl of pho steaming in front of the last. All women.

"We do hire men as well," Belinda said, shaking hands. "But not many."

"There's Carl," Willa corrected from behind Belinda's elbow.

"Chef Carl," Soo-Jin clarified.

Jamila and Kim, Scrapbooks/Crafts/Gifting Specialist and Gerontology Specialist respectively, kept eating. Jacqueline, Community Integration/Housing Specialist, nodded. And then Rosemary walked in with all her talk about teaching terrorists.

Earlier, in the interview, Rosemary warned Freddie she needed to answer only one question. "Now, wow me. I want your answer to be bold. Even sexy. Make it memorable."

Freddie did not giggle. Did not sweat profusely. *Sexy. Bold. I can do this.*

"In one sentence, tell me about the most interesting day of the most interesting job you've ever had."

Freddie knew that gardens, kids, and part-time waitressing didn't cut it. There'd been a bombing the day before at an embassy in Kuzbekistan. It was on NPR that morning as she was doing the drop-off and then again as she followed Rosemary's shiny red BMW. She'd been thinking about them. Wondering, as she often did, if they were all still alive. Her host family and former students. That answer was unknown, but she did know this answer for Rosemary. Still, it made her feel sick. The same story pulled out when needed. Her not quite "I once had a farm in Africa."

I once taught Emily Dickinson to terrorists.

Bold? Sexy? I know what you're thinking, but this was not the beginning of the century. The twenty-something lesbian drag thing didn't count. No big deal. Just as every NorCal lesbian her mother's age used to be married to a man, nearly every NorCal Mama Freddie's age was at one time or another a lesbian. Even if only for a week. As Willa said, they'd come of age in the time of Nancy Reagan, AIDS, and Kurt Cobain—isn't that what Willa said? *The Interesting Generation.* They'd been scared to death *and* pissed off. Kissing girls was the only interesting thing left for them to do in their twenties. Drag Kinging the King—even for a minister's daughter—was nothing compared to young terrorists.

Freddie knew what she had to say. Not completely true, not completely false, but it was the best answer. Her best answer. She would have to tell some of the story, again, here, in service to this one and only interview question. Freddie hadn't realized until that moment how much she wanted *this* job. How much she needed *this* job.

She got the job.

"We want to use all your skills," Rosemary Rafferty said. "You are exactly what The Outsourcers needs—a woman with experiences."

Women with experiences, Freddie remembered later driving to the first pick-up. That's all Freddie ever wanted, to be *Interesting*. And now, to be wanted for it! Paid! To be paid for being everything she (maybe) already was. She didn't even have to pretend to be someone else; she just had to be more . . . herself.

Right?

Freddie told her family that night over celebratory sushi/Trader Joe's shoestring fries: "This is just part-time. You are still my *real* job." But even she knew something had shifted. Freddie was wanted now, not just needed.

Life might never again be the same.

It was a new feeling for Freddie, this being wanted for her skills. She'd spent a lifetime underemployed. Mister couldn't grasp how paradigm shifting this was for Freddie. How could he? Tech people feel this way at birth. "Go for it," he said. "Get us closer to our goal."

Housing. It's all anyone talked about in Silicon Valley. They were a generation of middle-class families (well, the tech version of middle-class), unable to find homes. There just weren't enough places to live near the work. The few homes that were available were purchased immediately by investors in other countries to be used as rental properties, or by groups of newly vested twenty-somethings without children who could no longer afford San Francisco or Oakland. And you had to have a million just to buy a shack.

It's what the at-home moms talked about while they waited for elementary pick-up. There were six of them in total for the entire grade: a former flight attendant, a former anesthesiologist, a former attorney, a former marketing manager, a former news anchor, and Freddie.

"I can't go to any more open houses. Brian won't let me. He said we'd have to get stock in BevMo first. I just come home and cry and drink. It's that bad."

"It's worse," the former marketing manager complained. "I've seen every place up to two hours out. That's as far as the G-shuttle goes. Nothing. Well, unless we go in debt for the rest of our lives on an ugly, half-rotted house we'd have to tent immediately for termites."

"It's the smell that gets me," the former attorney sniffed.

"Of the bugs?"

"Of the houses."

These women huddled together, their faces serious with sorrow.

"You're the lucky one, Ji-ae. You bought before the bubble." They all smiled slightly at their elder, the former anesthesiologist, the only one of them lucky enough to have a mortgage.

"The second bubble," Ji-ae clarified.

"We will never save enough for a deposit, even—" and they all filled in the blank: *even if It goes public, even if They get another round of funding*, or *even with the RSUs*. These were women with families that received, periodically, what most Americans earned for an entire year. Tech stock was the hand of God. And still, it took years of saving to buy a 900-square-foot, million-plus condo. With no backyard. In a bad school district.

"What's the answer?" Freddie asked, keeping an eye on her youngest. She'd bought some extra time with a double-barreled granola bar.

"Rent forever."

"I'm sick of finding new rentals. Stability—"

"Doesn't exist here."

"It doesn't seem to matter how much you save. We can't even get in the game. Everything in Middlefield is gone. You were lucky to find a rental, Freddie. The waiting list is insane. My neighbors sold their place last week to a corporation in Beijing. And their house wasn't even 'for sale.'"

"Make Me Move," the women murmured in unison.

"Where *did* they move, though?" the former news anchor asked.

Everyone was waiting for the answer. These women who checked all the real estate websites weekly to see if there were any new pockets with houses and good enough schools where a tech shuttle might drive, any place with an equation that could possibly work.

"I don't even need *that* good of an API, you know." The women purposefully looked away from the school on whose grounds they were standing. It was their job to keep a 5 API school *good enough* by selling it to their neighbors. Most families in Middlefield sent their children to private school if they couldn't get into The Hub. These women were tasked with public relations for the *other* public school: *your brilliant children will be fine in a 5 API elementary, trust us.* The truth was, none of these women could afford any other option. They worked to make it all work.

"I don't know. We drove out about an hour. No, not Pleasanton, the other way. I mean look at us: mountains here, ocean there. Gorgeous weather. Jobs, of course. And as we were driving, I kept thinking, 'You know we could live out here, get a place, a little room to breathe.' But then we stopped and the people were, like, toothless. I mean it was real Carny Bob shit. We ordered an ahi salad. And, let me tell you, that was no ahi."

Their laughter faded into desperation as the bell rang. They grew quiet as they searched the incoming tide for their children.

"I never thought I'd still be renting in my forties," the former flight attendant sighed. "Hey, who's that?"

They all turned to watch a woman dressed in matched clothes bound out of an illegally parked SUV. She stepped as if to a soundtrack. Her hair brushed, makeup on.

"It's the new family that moved in last week," Ji-ae said. "She came from Ohio or somewhere around there. Why didn't you look that sharp when you arrived, Freddie?" They all smiled. Freddie rolled her eyes. "She probably had a four bedroom with a yard back there."

"With a pantry and a 10 school. She looks so hopeful, doesn't she? She doesn't know yet. This is the Peninsula. Say goodbye to Ohio."

"But we've got all the jobs," the former attorney sighed. "You know she left a mega mansion. For 300,000 Ohio dollars. Poor thing. 2.5 here, baby."

"Easily. With swamp smell."

"In a bad district."

"An hour out, at least."

"But we've got jobs," the former news anchor sniffed. "All the jobs you could ever want! Welcome to Middlefield."

three

"Ben?" Freddie repeated. But her client was no longer paying attention. He was fiddling with his phone. His earpiece already in.

"You wouldn't be able to use the executive report to handle status. You can do a—ah—review easily, just like you're doing an MBO. Just create a new type. And that will work. It won't require any more of the system." Ben lifted up his first finger. Pointer. "You're just basically doing an almost exactly . . . or an exactly MBO kind of thing."

He crouched over the table. Half standing. He was no longer telling Freddie about the time when he was climbing in Puerto Rico and his hand slipped. He was not talking about his philosophy concerning the difference between the books he *should* read and the books he *might* read (or not); the films he *should* see and the films he *did* see (or not). His voice wasn't just hard now. It was mocking.

"What is it you're trying to accomplish? Because I don't get it." Ben stood. "Just a minute. Hey, um, Freddie, back here later? Text me." He was already walking away. Freddie began a note to Belinda: *RE: Our shared client, Ben Bhattacharya. Multitasking Manners - Possible discussion topic?*

Freddie flicked through her phone. She had Seti next. Seti's nanny would be picking the children up from school about now. Seti's children went to private school, STEM-focused, year-round in Palo Alto. The school offered flex-time to the students; they could come and go as they liked, school was the constant. So Seti's children had piano lessons on

Monday mornings, Mandarin on Wednesday afternoons, and Freddie on Thursdays for lunchtime gardening (organic, heirloom if possible). Ballet and swimming on Saturdays. Freddie supposed they had Sunday off.

Her phone lit up with another text message:

Mister: *Bad news. Our rent is going up again* Mister: *So just chked around. Everyones is* Mister: *There is no place else to go! Everything else is double/triple* Mister: *Cupertino, Los Altos, Sunnyvale, SJ even = INSANE* Mister: *Did u call specialist*

Freddie waited for the … and it never came. Freddie: *Tried. Was on hold for too long. Trying again now.* That was almost a lie. She would try later.

Freddie headed to her car. Today they would be harvesting radishes, taste-testing their own pickled vegetables, and making homemade bahn mi sandwiches. And then Seti's children would return to school, and Freddie would return for a few more minutes with Ben before her own life began again. There was something she needed to remember and couldn't. What was she forgetting? Rosemary's mantra—KEEP MY ATTENTION! No, that wasn't it, but Freddie wrote KMA on a Post-it beside her steering wheel. It kept falling.

Freddie's client, Pamela Ramos-Wu, called crying just as Freddie turned the corner. "But I wanted to be that woman. My neighbor stays home. I see her sometimes on the weekends. She bakes cookies and they put up these decorations on the window." *So you live by me*, Freddie thought. A joke Freddie would never tell. They both needed to pretend that Pam was the most important thing to Freddie, that Freddie had nothing but Pam in her life.

If Pam saw Freddie's house, if Pam saw Freddie at Costco with her kids, if Pam actually knew Freddie, the illusion would be gone. Freddie wouldn't be a professional anymore. She'd just be someone's mom, somebody like Pam's neighbor who always seemed to have extra cupcake liners and put up doily hearts the first week of February. "I just can't be stuck at home."

"I understand," Freddie said. It was the truth. *My life barely passes the Bechdel test. And I can't tell you that.* It would break the fundamental rule of The Outsourcers if Freddie shared with Pamela her own experiences, her own fast-tracked marriage (*we're in love, we're in our thirties, why the hell not?*)

and surprisingly quick pregnancy.

We didn't have a clue, Freddie thought.

"We had no idea what we were in for," Mister now said regularly.

Bach Drops weren't going to cut it, but nothing else would either.

"I need to go, Freddie. Just got a call."

The screen on Freddie's phone went black.

Keep My Attention. The notes were everywhere that last week of the month of Remember. That time when Freddie was racing to finish her own memoir—what would become her first of many. *KMA*, thought Freddie. She was counting them, an assignment given by Rosemary. She did a search in her backup drive for *sex*. She had to make a tally.

A memoir needed to be specific.

Just another set of stories told in the beginning—their sexual histories—shared between actual sex in a too small bed. All while establishing their own story, which became primary only after the fact.

Freddie and her Mister met multiple times before it stuck. Friends of friends, a string of parties, reintroductions, and some truly great conversations. The joke was that they both brought a new date to each of these parties—never the same person, consistently someone more boring than bad—but then they always seemed to meet each other in the kitchen with that party's date nearby.

They talked about his job and what brought him to Indiana—*"My friend's start-up. Temporary."* They talked about what brought Freddie back to Indiana—*"I was evacuated from a terrorist cell. I'm teaching here now. For the time being."*

And then, one party, they'd both arrived solo. It was Halloween. He was concerned because he didn't want Freddie to think he couldn't find a date. Freddie was concerned because she'd brought an Indian guy as a date the first time they'd met and she didn't want him to think she had a thing for Indian men.

"She has a thing for Indians," came their mutual friend's warning as the future Mister tried, unsuccessfully, not to obviously linger in the kitchen. He wasn't waiting. *Exactly.*

"That's okay," he answered, pouring another whiskey as he kept himself from staring at Freddie. "I'm the least Indian Indian on the planet.

I'm Canadian for god's sake."

"You're Indian for Indiana," their friend laughed. "It's too bad really. People gonna hate on you if you go after Freddie."

"Come on," he laughed smugly. "I'm sure another single guy will drop into the community here soon enough."

"You don't understand, man. Freddie's democratic. She's been out with Indian women too. Look at her." Their friend laughed, watching Freddie dance with the head of the philosophy department to a Talking Heads song. "Careful, man. You just might fall in love."

That night the future Mister used *juxtapose* in his boarding school accent. He was cyclist thin with cut glass cheekbones. He was dressed like Einstein, but the wig had gotten itchy. Freddie was dressed as Sherlock Holmes but with Jennifer Aniston hair.

It was easy. Simple. He was real. She was make believe. They were both more than ready. The prescribed gender roles were even simpler to fall into. At first, it was almost a joke between them. They were made for each other.

But the fault lines?

They'd talked about everything in the beginning in that too small bed. Of course, Freddie was more embarrassed about her specialization in Partition Literature, those bindi *and* mehndi pics, and all that damn yoga—her *colonialism*—than anything else. And he was more concerned about the way she saw him, about how she perceived his strengths, than any lacking he might also own. But that was the beginning.

As their lives grew so did their bed. Named for where they'd finally come to reside, this King and Queen of the great state of California, their bed wide and their fault lines, in that valley between them, another something left unspoken.

Freddie left Seti's with just enough time to head back for Ben Part Two. *If* he was on time. *If* he didn't blue screen. She had an hour before the first pick-up of her own life.

"You're going to be so proud of me," Ben said before sitting down. Freddie knew he was in a better mood. He'd ditched the morning cardigan and was wearing his favorite *Meet me on the Playa* shirt.

If truth be told, Ben Bhattacharya was one of Freddie's favorite clients. He had enormous grey eyes, a slumpy walk, and a round, babyish face his mummy and aunties still kissed. They met weekly at Chronos-Coffee, around the corner from HackerSpace and down the street from Ben's newest startup. They never met at HackerSpace—Ben was adamant, and Freddie understood his desire for complete compartmentalization. Anyway, the baristas at Chronos kept a few tables on the far side near the fence. These tables were set apart from the entry, with no outlets and lousy free Google WiFi. They were always empty.

"I've been reading," he said. Ben didn't pull out a screen. He pulled out a book. "I made notes in the margins like you suggested." And then, remembering: "Oh. I'm sorry about before."

Ben recently turned thirty. He usually traveled in packs. He wanted a long-term girlfriend, not a wife. His first startup was acquired by Google years ago. He was one of the original Facebook fifty: Employee #22. His last two startups tanked. He'd hired Freddie to make him "better."

"It's thoughtful of you to apologize." Freddie would make another note for Belinda, but knew not to tread on her colleague's work. Belinda's job was charm. Belinda worked with Ben twice a week. Freddie's tasks with Ben were slightly more nebulous, but one was distinct. They read books together. "So, tell me, what do you think?"

She had her own copy in front of her.

"I like it," he said. "If you take your time, it's funny even."

"Yes." Freddie was pleased but tried not to read *too pleased*. Not just yet. "Remember Virginia Woolf . . ."

"From a couple months ago?"

"Yes." Freddie nodded. "She said, about this book, that it was 'one of the few English novels written for grown-ups.' I'm paraphrasing."

They both held copies of *Middlemarch*.

"You're starting to consider me a grown-up." Ben's face reddened. "A very good thing."

Oh, Freddie thought. *Oh, no.*

"And your date? Let's talk about that. How did it go?" She opened her book and grabbed for her pen as if somehow prepared to take notes.

"It was pretty good." Ben nodded, his face grim. "You were right. She was super impressed that I'd read Scarlett Thomas. But I almost slipped and called her Scarlett O'Hare." Ben laughed, showing his ridiculously straight teeth. He'd once told Freddie that he sometimes had to wear a teeth guard during the late afternoon. *Stress grinding*, he'd called it, blushing. Freddie returned his smile. Maybe this was all just about Ben learning. It was a process, wasn't it? For all of us. She just needed to keep him focused. Keep his attention—correctly focused.

She told herself that this was the Ben that was easy to market. The sweet Ben. The one she sometimes felt she was pulling in a red wagon, up a hill. Freddie couldn't shake the feeling that Ben reminded her of someone. She glanced again at his eyes, his curls, and those straight suburban teeth.

"Scarlett O'Hara," Freddie prompted. She never used "my dear." Even with her children. That was a Rosemary, a Willa.

Willa—prime example of a voice masking a person's true self, Freddie thought, remembering. That time, over a year ago, when Freddie was sighing at the Round Table. Freddie felt stuck. She was weary of visiting a past she knew she wasn't capturing. Desperate to detach again and release, she just wanted to be finished. "I'm just not a memoir sort of person."

"You're exactly a memoir sort of person." Willa laughed, walking into the break room. "Another now skinny, yoga posing, Whole Foods shopping mummy."

"I am not skinny." Freddie was huffy.

Willa had been answering phones. Her voice tinny. She poured hot water into her thin cup. "Rosemary told me you'd decided on a title." Was that a smirk?

"So what's the title going to be?" Belinda asked, positioning herself as a fence of kindness between Willa and Freddie.

"It's an embarrassing story actually," Freddie began. "As a kid I filled journals full of possible book titles. Movie titles too." She cleared her throat, surprised to find everyone around the table still listening. She avoided all possible eye contact with Willa.

"Anyway, I made a notation of one and it just stuck: *The Roof of Life*. I believe I wrote down, 'Sex lies at the roof of life, and when you learn how to . . . I don't know, *negotiate* is the wrong word entirely . . . but when you learn about sex, you learn about life.' It seemed such a beautiful image, at least to my twelve-year-old self who knew *nothing* about sex that wasn't in literature. The *roof* of life, the connection." Freddie's fingertips touched. "Safety and comfort. Well, anyway—I attributed the quote to Octavio Paz." Freddie shook her head. "And, of course, it also seemed like something Lady Brett would say in *The Sun Also Rises*."

They were still listening, so Freddie continued, looking sheepishly at the various mugs and water bottles that sat on the table between them.

"But in the process of this last month, I discovered that I'd made a mistake. I'm not sure which self did it." Freddie's face flushed. "First, there was a spelling error. It wasn't *roof* but *root*. Which is an entirely different image. Basically, I messed the whole thing up." Freddie laughed. "It wasn't even Octavio Paz. It was Havelock Ellis."

"Sex lies at the *root* of life, and we can never learn to reverence life until we know how to understand sex," Willa quoted in her most beautiful tone.

"Yes," Freddie said. She nodded and finally looked at Willa. Willa's face was quite serious. Not sneering or smirking. And then, Willa turned and left the room.

"So, which title did you choose?" Soo-Jin was proving her attention span.

"*The Roof of Life*," Freddie said. "You see, the mistake was mine and I just kept repeating it. Those four words. A complete error, but I never knew that. I mean, I didn't even look it up until now. The Internet didn't exist for most of it. But still, it was mine, my mistake."

No one was listening now. Phones were nestled in palms. People were still nodding and smiling, but email was being checked. Texts were sent in that moment. A calendar was updated. Freddie was staring at the table but thinking of a view on a very lonely night of a valley filled with tin rooftops. No electricity. Lights twinkling from kerosene lamps. A drum beating out on the breeze. That night, Freddie had looked out as she hovered over her journal, tears pooling, wondering if this might be her Roof of Life.

It was not. It was just one roof of her life.

Freddie felt, at the end of that month of remembering, so much empathy with her twenty-seven-year-old version. Yes, she had been entirely self-absorbed, so unthinking, filled with such odd fears and worries, but that's why Freddie loved her. *You are not alone. You are just fine. Make things and worry less*, Freddie would tell that younger girl. *I have discovered that I love her*, Freddie wanted to say out loud now as she sat at The Outsourcers Round Table.

"That girl I was, she was just figuring out her narrative. She didn't believe in happy endings." Freddie had been feeling brave until that last bit. *Happy? Content? Full? And "ending" was the wrong word entirely.* Freddie looked around the room relieved no one was watching her, no one listening. "Back to work," Freddie said, standing.

As she walked out the door, heading to her next client, Willa said it. At first, Freddie thought Willa was speaking to someone on the phone. It didn't seem to make sense. "What name are you using, my dear?"

When Freddie still didn't answer, Willa continued, "Rosemary told me you were considering Anonymous. My dear, we've come too far to return to that. Haven't we, Freddie?"

"It's not that," Freddie began. "We don't use full names and it just feels odd to only be using one name and so I thought—"

"A happy ending for Anonymous then?"

"I never *meant* that a happy ending equals a husband and two children in California. I don't believe that."

Willa was silent.

"A happy ending has always just been about love, about connection. A sentimental thought, but perhaps we need more sentiment." Maybe when everyone walks out at the end of The End, that's what we'll all hope for. It sounded to Freddie like something Hugh Grant would say in a voiceover. "I did my best."

"Once again, putting the *Me* in memoir. I admit, I was hoping for better." And as if to herself, Willa muttered, "I patently never trust the first person."

"It could have happened to any young woman then," Freddie heard herself saying.

"Exactly," Willa said. "Which makes it even more absurd. Your generation all think you could have been something better than you actually are. Self-loathing and deep solipsism marry to create an id beyond ids."

Later, Freddie revised this discussion in her head. Willa should have said, "Ethan Hawke," and then Freddie could have said, "Ethan Hawke—I love him." Willa, "Enough said." And they'd laugh. End scene.

Cue Music.

But instead, Willa asked, "What are you afraid of? There is a level of fear in everything you do. And you've not given yourself that step away for completion, at least in this draft. It seems to me to be the ultimate act in narcissism. The love affair with one's own past and then, after all of that, not owning it. Very odd, indeed, but then, you're one of *those* people."

"What people?" Freddie was almost too afraid to find out.

"The all or nothing sort." Willa shook her head.

"Rosemary said she wanted something with"—the embarrassment to hear the actual words coming out of her mouth was almost too much to bear—"a sexy, angsty quality." *At least I have the decency to blush*, Freddie narrated to herself.

"The proverbial sex, drugs, and young terrorists. But, Freddie, that's obviously not *your* story."

"I had a month to write it."

"I'm suggesting nothing more," Willa said. "Or less."

That brief moment of reward for the sheer effort of creation dissipated in a flash. Freddie felt hollow; worse than that, she felt absurd. Willa actually got up out of her seat. She leaned against the beautiful wood of her dominion, that vast counter where she ruled, her bob swinging forward. "Freddie, a piece of advice—my dear, find the middle."

But it took a year for Freddie to remember Willa's warning. Neither roof, nor root, but the middle. *What about the middle?* Willa's words came back to Freddie as she sat across from Ben, another memoir in motion.

I can't, Freddie thought. *KMA*, she reminded herself.

"Let's start with that time you nearly fell in Puerto Rico. How did the rock wall feel?" Freddie wanted to know because she needed to write that moment for Ben. That moment of all or nothing, when hands and feet gripped something stronger than he would ever be. And that moment when they stopped. When all that was left was air.

four

Freddie expected the prophesied *End of the World* to be like any other Friday, at least any of the recent Fridays. She'd written so many memoirs-for-hire, she could barely keep track of them, but she'd gotten them down to a two-week cycle. Freddie knew what to ask and how to ask it. They were usually only about 50,000 words. She liked to turn them in on Fridays and then take the family out for Mexican.

Earlier, she'd pressed send on an Apple guy's memoir about the motorcycle trip he'd taken across Australia. Next week, Freddie was starting a new one—job at Facebook, no kids, queer, biohacker, descendant of a Mormon saint.

"You're made for this one," Rosemary said during their five-minute weekly meet-up over FaceTime. This sentence alone led Freddie to wonder once again if Rosemary *had* actually read her memoir. The more likely scenario was that Rosemary had asked Willa to share some of the highlights. "Now, here's the situation, my dear. The client wants it faster than fast. I think a birthday is involved. And she wants some sort of low-tech interactive element."

"What does that mean, exactly?" Freddie asked, packing lunches.

"She wants some of your magic. Inspire us. She's paying to have it letter-pressed." Rosemary stopped for a moment. "Freddie, you understand how well you're doing with all these memoirs, don't you? I think we should chat about an incentive. Why not drive into the office? Our five minutes is sadly up. Oh, and Happy End of the World, my dear! The ancients were something, weren't they?"

And then came the call from the doctor's office after Freddie's last drop-off. She'd just turned the Motown off. Motown meant drop-off and pick-up: *signed, sealed, delivered, I'm yours*. Freddie was just pulling out of the preschool's parking lot, already picturing a scene in her client's grandmother's kitchen. *Paper dolls, of course!* Her client's wearable sensor beneath her left ear—when the phone rang in the passenger seat. The sound startled her. Freddie kept the ringer on loud while the kids were away from her.

That's the thing. It had all gotten too cute.

It's illegal to pick up a phone in the car while driving in California, but Freddie was already stuck in roadwork, officially halted. The number on the screen was unfamiliar. Freddie answered. Watch her. Look at her eyes.

"Yes, this is his mother speaking. Sure. We can come in. When?"

That moment. There. When she heard herself figuring out the "best time" to get in the doctor's office that day, around her work, around the school schedule; that's when Freddie knew.

Oh.

She'd forgotten. She'd gotten comfortable. Complacent. She'd become a person who bought small appliances and worried about happiness. She'd become someone who hurried so she could run that last errand between work and pick-up, between pick-up and piano or soccer. A world where time could be controlled. She stared out the windshield. Caution. The orange cones. The signs. *Stop!* The guy in the hard hat flipped from *Stop* to *Slow*.

She hated making this phone call.

The first try her husband let go to voicemail. He was probably in a meeting. Her phone beeped. *In mtg Do u need something*, read the text. *Please call me*, she typed back.

Freddie parked at the 7/11 a block from their neighborhood. She could see the Middlefield sign through the windshield. It was made of stone. The sign was the only thing in the entire neighborhood made of stone. Freddie imagined it crumbling to dust when the Big One hit.

The 7/11 cash machine didn't charge them a fee, and Freddie needed cash for Maribel next Saturday so Freddie could hit her client's deadline and for the house cleaners next week. The occasional house cleaning and sitter hours were Freddie's big treats since starting at The Outsourcers. Freddie's Midwestern reticence shifted when she'd come home to a sparkling house she hadn't had to scrub. For the first time in her life, Freddie was on the other side of the mop. *This is heaven*, she thought. But, being Freddie, she also liked to think of it as providing an income, *work*, for others—a kind of good deed. And Freddie always made sure that her children had chores, telling them, repeatedly, that *she* used to clean houses and businesses, that *she* used to take care of other people's children for work.

"It is an important job," Freddie told her children. "And we need to always remember that and help in any way we can." But it wasn't an *important* job; Freddie knew that. A *useful* job, a *helpful* job—but the only person it was really important to was Freddie.

"The Marias" who cleaned were actually Luz Adoncia and Elena-Jessenia Manolita, but they knew their clients were too white to deal with proper pronunciation, so they just went by "Maria." And what did "The Marias" think of Freddie? That story could begin with the time Freddie offered to drop dinner off after their surgery last summer. They were explaining that they couldn't work the following month. But Freddie wasn't sure if it was Luz's surgery or Elena-Jessenia's or if they both were getting surgeries. Freddie's Spanish was much worse than their English, but she understood it was a hysterectomy.

No more babies. No más bebés.

"Can I bring you some dinner?" Freddie asked, her own children pulling on her. "Puedo traer la cena?"

"No," Luz answered, walking up the stairs. "We don't need food. We need Windex, not this vinegar."

Maribel was different. Freddie *knew* Maribel. They'd met at the park Freddie's first year in California, chatting over grapes and crackers—Freddie was friends with all the nannies. If one friend can work for another?

Friend, Boss, Work, Job.

But this was only information, the life stored behind what was happening through Freddie's phone, a life already in revision.

"Fucking genetics," her husband was saying. "I hate that he has to deal with this. You can't understand how much I hate this."

"I know," Freddie answered. "He was just getting back to . . ." She wouldn't say it. She would not. *We were all getting back to life.* "Listen, I know you have that big release today—" But she was thinking about fault and genetics and how she couldn't protect any of them, not really.

She stared at the rain. One week of rain a year. *It was the rain*, she decided. And there had been yet another school shooting and all those poor children, the same age, the same exact grade as her daughter. And the radio kept talking about the End of the World and ancient prophecies that were making everyone bring up the old millennium fears and list reasons to either party or hide in a bunker. Nothing made sense.

It was the dumb things too. Like schedules and the way no one seemed to be talking but everyone was yelling or sullen or afraid. The memoirs were fine, but Freddie was sick of writing all the posts and feeds in other people's voices: *Anyone else feeling freaked by the Uniqlo blimp overhead?#ya'llgettinalil'HungerGamesonme?*

Even the stupid life questions, about value and purpose and reality— *Bullshit.* None of it mattered now. Everything faded away except her son and her daughter and what was about to happen. The End of the World was nigh.

"I'm going with you," her husband said, his voice louder through the phone.

"Really?"

"Don't say it like that."

"I didn't mean it like you think," she answered. "I meant that I'm grateful. Thank you."

She loved him. Not just because he was going with them to the appointment, but also because he was the kind of man who never said, *I told you so.* The last two surgeries hadn't done the job. They would need another. They would do this. They were a good team. It could all end up okay.

After Freddie hung up, her phone rang again. She didn't recognize the number. Didn't care. It would go to voicemail.

Freddie was in the passenger seat now, everything postponed. Her husband driving, their son in his car seat in the back. "We're just going for another check," they told him, picking him up too early. His lunchbox still full, their smiles betraying them; voices shiny. "You remember Dr. Timmy." Their boy had just turned three. One. Two. Three. Surgeries.

"Daddy coming?" he asked from the back.

"Daddy's never been to Dr. Timmy's and he wants to visit the trains with you." She stopped. "I mean, Daddy's been to the hospital with us, but he hasn't been to an appointment and he wants to go."

Freddie's phone rang again. Messages piling up.

"The tables have turned." Mister squeezed her leg, looking at her phone. And then, in a whisper: "Your shit's blowing up."

"It's a client. I'll make it quick. *Hello*—" Freddie knew she sounded annoyed. It was unprofessional.

"We need to talk."

"Good morning, Angela." Freddie, recognizing the voice, returned to the same tone she'd just used for her son. "How can I help you?"

"They are not preparing her enough at school."

"I'm very happy to refer you to my colleague Soo-Jin. She is our Education Specialist at . . ." Freddie almost smiled. She sounded a little like Willa just then.

"No. You know what happened at that school yesterday? They aren't preparing them enough here. I need you to create a, I don't know, more personalized version . . . My daughter's school is right along the trail."

My daughter's school is right along the trail too, Freddie wanted to say. "I understand your fears," Freddie said, instead.

"I can't focus at work. I'm having nightmares. I just need this to be . . . better. You know?"

"Of course." Of course Freddie knew. Her husband was pulling into the hospital parking lot. *Get off the phone*. Freddie was no longer listening to Angela's voice. *Stay in the car*, she thought. Freddie wanted to tell her husband to keep driving. They could stop at the school, pick up their girl, and just leave. They'd go somewhere else and leave everything behind. No more surgeries. No more virtual jobs. No more anything. They'd fish and drink out of coconuts and wear the same clothes until they disintegrated. No more grocery lists. No more anniversary cards to mail. No more phones.

"I can send you in for me." Angela was still talking. "Okay, I know this isn't politically correct, you know, but her school's really . . . *mixed*. I'd like you to assess both outside and internal factors. I mean, you know, it's often classmates that do this."

She'd written Angela's holiday letter and did some ghostposting on her Facebook page, but Freddie didn't remember the family. There had been too many of them now. Too many babies and children playing violin and tennis nearly-semi-pro. Something made her ask. "And what is the age range?"

"Sorry?"

"What grade level are we studying?" Her husband had stopped the car. The doors unlocked. He and their son were semi-whispering about a red Tesla that passed.

"Oh, right," Angela answered. "Kindergarten."

Rosemary didn't even tell Freddie in person. She sent a text: *Can u mt tmrw? (can't bring kids) Exciting news! 11:00. Not at office. Willa sending location/GPS now.*

Freddie texted back: *No kidcare. Sorry.*

But Freddie wasn't sorry. She was sick of "exciting news." She didn't care anymore about anything. She just wanted her own together under the same roof, no one but the four of them, nothing but each other. Her son was scheduled for surgery. The last one had been especially tough on him, the recovery excruciating. Last year's "miracle" proven to be yet another dud.

She built a timeline in her head. Months ago, he'd started saying again that his foot hurt, pointing to his hip, and she kept thinking it would somehow get better if she didn't make a big deal, if she kept up the massage and the night braces. Growing pains, even? But then he began to roll it again sometimes after preschool, go high on his tiptoes when he was tired, and one time she actually caught herself saying, "Try and walk like this."

Bad mother. Good father. He saw the truth. She would just have to get them through another surgery. She would stop working. She would be there. She would heal him. She would give up anything for them to be safe. It wasn't—but it also was—her fault. She'd taken her eye off the ball. She'd gotten a little happy. A little consumed. She'd forgotten.

Another text from Rosemary: *Bringing Willa to hang with kiddos. Need you there. Sorry.*

Freddie remembered saying it. "We're one of the lucky ones," she said to her husband, on the way home from the last pre-op appointment. He went to all the appointments with them now.

All the other children waiting—watching the static-y, now vintage Pixar—were children in masks. They were bald. Children encased. And not just their feet; metal shells encased their bodies. Children in wheelchairs with IVs and syringes and oxygen. Children accustomed to waiting rooms. Children with parents who needed a translator. Parents who arrived with bags of food and clothes, prepared to wait it out. Parents who took the bus with three kids to the hospital to wait in this room, knowing there was no way to pay.

"That money you made from doing the ebook." He didn't even call it a memoir.

"I know," she said. "We just had it there, waiting. It'll cover our portion, plus some. We're one of the lucky ones."

Who needs a house? Freddie wasn't even sure she really wanted a house. She knew she was supposed to want a house for them. It was her job to give them the illusion of stability. But they had a place to live. They paid an ungodly sum every month. Anyone would love to live in their townhome.

In the car, they used to play a kind of game, the conversation on an everlasting repeat. She'd say, What about Portland? And Mister would say, Not enough jobs, better house prices. Fun. Austin is still on the list? Definitely. Awesome rides. North Carolina? Suburbs.

They would go on like this for entire drives, rating all the tech hubs, major and minor, home and abroad. They would look through Trulia on Sunday nights and talk about the square footage, and then she would look at tiny house blogs to reassure herself that they weren't becoming someone else.

She'd gotten greedy. Why had she done this, this wanting? A home didn't matter. *You always just have to leave*, Freddie thought. We all do, don't we, at some point. No, she wouldn't think about that. What was ownership anyway? She'd always been against ownership. It was about community. Quality of life. The surgery was scheduled for the following week. Freddie had already emailed Rosemary for a leave of absence. Her family needed her. Never forget—"We're one of the lucky ones."

five

The sign beside the door read: MemCorps™.

The office was located in a walkup between a Chinese herbalist and a gelato shop in downtown Mountain View. Freddie disliked coming into the town on weekdays around lunchtime. Castro Street at 11:00 a.m. on a Wednesday was full of hungry Googlers wanting off campus. It was the looks that bothered her. People in town at that time of day hated the stroller, hated her jeans and sneakers, and occasionally, even sent hateful glances to the kid in the triceratops hat. How was that even possible? It went against Darwinism, Survival of the Cutest. Freddie looked down at her son's head and pushed the button. "We'll be so quick," she said as the door clicked. Freddie and her boy walked up the thin stairs slowly, hand-in-hand, dragging the stroller behind them.

Yesterday was his last day at preschool before the surgery, his last day of Normal until he recovered. She'd made cupcakes for him to take in, the icing not the color of doctor's scrubs but a cheerful, pale yellow.

This was also Freddie's last day of Normal, and she resented the fact that she was spending it with people she didn't even want to see. She wanted to go home. But Willa was waiting at the top of the stairs with an enormous apple juice box, organic bunny crackers, a bag full of new coloring books and a ludicrously perfect box of crayons. Then, from behind her back, Willa pulled—"BrandnewMatchboxsetoffiveEmergencyVehicles!" the kid shrieked. Willa knew exactly what to get. For some reason this shocked Freddie. Her worn-out Timbuktu bag filled with half-eaten items in Ziplocs and broken crayons was immediately forgotten. Freddie was forgotten. *My dear*, indeed.

"I'll be right in here, sweetie." *Why was she talking like that?* Freddie was saying it to herself. It was a glass door. She could see Rosemary smiling at her, motioning her in towards a long maple table with people smiling around it, looking at her above laptops, a gigantic monitor behind them. A man got up and walked towards the door, waving at her, an enormous grin on his face. Freddie didn't recognize him. Silver hair, tanned, handsome, maybe a year or two older than her parents. She wondered if he was Rosemary's . . . guy? (They'd all wondered at the office. Willa never said a word, even after wine. There were bets. Soo-Jin thought younger. Belinda thought older or dead. Jamila thought Al Gore.) This man and Rosemary did seem to coordinate: confident, wealthy, silvery, expensive-casual.

"What a handsome chap you walked in with," the man boomed. "Thank you so much for coming today, Freddie. I know it's an inconvenience. Some coconut water? Matcha?"

He was beaming at Freddie, his hand on her arm, leading her through the door, letting it shut behind them, walking her into the room to that table and those people with laptops. Laptops either sleek silver or covered in stickers, everything seemingly in service to the enormous flat-screen monitor behind them. And in that minute, Freddie just wanted to turn and scoop up her baby boy and run as fast as she could down those thin steps. She could bust through the door if she had to. They didn't need to be here. They could be home, like usual, eating soup, watching *Sesame Street*, nibbling fruit cut into small bites, an eye on the clock so they could nap and wake up and go get their big girl on time.

He would be okay. He would have the surgery and he would recover and everything would be okay. Freddie kept moving, letting her arm be held, her back guided. She knew this guy. Didn't she?

Rosemary was giving her the client smile. "Freddie, I'd love for you to meet Marco Villatoni."

That's why.

"Freddie,"—that voice!—"I feel like I already know you."

"The feeling is mutual, Mr. Villatoni." At least that's what Freddie thought came out of her mouth. What she was thinking was HOLYSHIT!

Marco Villatoni, a bigger NPR star than Garrison Keillor, Ira Glass, Click and Clack, and Terri Gross combined. Marco Villatoni, The Voice of NPR's *Stories*, which—for decades—offered people the chance to share that moment of their lives of Before and After.

Freddie listened to *Stories* every Friday night of her childhood. She stayed up late, after *Washington Week in Review* and *Wall Street Week in Review* with Louis Rukeyser and his dollar bill hair, for that moment when PBS went off and NPR came on: "Welcome to *Stories*. I'm Marco Villatoni."

Just hearing Marco Villatoni say her name.

"Before we begin, Freddie," Rosemary said, holding out a screen, "please give us your signature. Just a simple NDA."

Freddie took the screen. It was a similar NDA to the one Rosemary used at The Outsourcers. Freddie signed her name.

"This is big, my dear." Rosemary smiled at the screen. "Let me introduce you now to everyone." She was almost purring. "We're bringing you into a paradigm shift here, Freddie. Let me be clear, we're changing the world in this room. Here we have—" and Rosemary rattled off several names. Everyone, in addition to Rosemary and Marco, consisted of three men and a woman. But Freddie was surprised when Rosemary introduced the man closest to the monitor as "Rajat."

"We've met." Rajat's face flushed, his hand up in a kind of wave. "Hello again, Freddie."

Everyone but Freddie stared at an inanimate object. She'd written a memoir for this man about his childhood in Alabama. When was it? Last winter? He'd called himself something else. He said he knew Ben through HackerSpace. That's where he and Freddie met. Where they'd spent well over a month on his memoir. His book was quite possibly the best she'd written. He had the very same Atari stickers on his laptop, but his name was different. Surya—what was his last name? Mohan? Mohani?

"We needed some inside information, as it were," Rosemary explained. "Rajat simply used a different name. Moving on. Let's begin the presentation. Rajat?"

"Basically, we've created an intelligent Life Navigator using what we call Creative Fact." Rajat handed out embossed MemCorps™ folders. Everyone opened his or hers but Freddie.

"I'm sorry," Freddie interrupted. Every time she looked in Surya/Rajat's direction, he flushed deeper. "Was that even your story? Growing up in Alabama? Or was it all a lie?"

"Freddie." Rosemary leaned forward. "Tone, please."

"You knew about this?" Freddie was angry. She didn't really care about her tone. "Rosemary?"

"The only *lie*, if you want to call it that, was my name," Rajat began. "And. Okay. I found you. It wasn't an accident. I struck up a conversation with a few of your clients. I spent some time researching how you went about your . . . process. All to help our progress." Rajat held up his palms. "Can I continue?"

Marco nodded.

"You've created another Siri." Freddie knew she sounded pissed. Rosemary wouldn't look at her.

"Actually, we've taken it a step further. Do you know anything about Richard Feynman? He was—"

"A theoretical physicist." This was the "Surya" Freddie remembered. He was an ass. He just had a good story. Freddie would stare him down if she had to. "*Surely, You're Joking . . .*"

"Excuse me?"

"One of Feynman's books," another guy at the table said. "*Surely You're Joking, Mister Feynman!*"

"Or, another favorite, *What Do You Care What Other People Think*." Freddie sighed. It was a first for Freddie. Never before had she said exactly the right thing at the right moment. She felt it. The power. She looked over at her son's triceratops hat through the glass door, at his face; he was telling Willa something. It was a joke. Freddie knew the way his face looked when he told a joke. She watched Willa react. Watched her put her hand to her mouth and laugh. Willa was good.

"Basically, we've taken his theories about time and created a model using daily output. So, not only tracking how humans deal with the Four Ds, but what their varied responses could be or could have been. A kind of alternate history function, if you will."

"Our dream come true." Marco smiled. "All of the specifics combined and accessible. Captured human responses. The literature of life as a guide to our everyday existence."

"The Four Ds?" Freddie wished she'd asked for coffee.

"Disaster, Distress, Displacement, and Disease," Marco counted on his fingers. "You're a mother; you understand the concerns we have globally for our future, our children's future. The world is a mess. Crisis situations abound, refugees, environmental issues beyond imagination, terror, pathogens, nuclear war. Hell, meteors from space." Rajat and one of the other men snickered. "We have created something which not only captures responses but also projects the alternatives."

It took Freddie a minute. "You're tracking their lives and their alternate lives." A statement, not a question. "A kind of—"

"Collective Cognition," Rajat interrupted.

"AI," Freddie said.

"I told you she'd get it quickly." Rosemary nodded. "This is big, Freddie."

And that's when it dawned on Freddie that Rosemary seemed to know everything that was happening. Not just about the memoirs, but all of it. Had Rosemary planned all of this? Rajat/Surya seemed to know Ben. But then everyone in Silicon Valley knew Ben. Was this why Rosemary began providing the memoir service for her clients in the first place? Because she knew that their future was tied to this program? To MemCorps™? Is this why Rosemary had Freddie write her memoir in a month (faster is always better in the Valley), making a piece of Freddie's personal history downloadable for eternity?

Alternate lives? Those two words. Multiplied to infinity. And beyond.

Freddie wasn't listening. She needed to listen.

"But we've taken it a step further." Marco grinned. "She passed the Turing Test."

"She?" Everyone was smiling. It made Freddie want to scowl.

"You were so representative of your generation, we named our beta model after you."

"I always called Freddie our Superheroine," Rosemary murmured.

"Speaking of 'Freddie,' why don't we meet her." Marco was already looking at the big flat-screen monitor.

"Your story—" began the other woman at the table. *Kelly?*—unless they were lying about her name too.

"*Memoir*." Marco nodded.

"—Yes. It hit each of our search terms." This seemed to mean a heck of a lot to Kelly.

Freddie made a list in her head of the possible terms they'd used. Life not only in multiple choice but with multiple answers, multiplied. Freddie thought of all her different selves. "Labels."

"No, search terms. They're fluid."

Rosemary was right. This was big. *Listen.* Freddie tried to make herself focus. *Stop looking through the door. Stop looking at his hat, at his face. Listen to what they're saying.*

"In addition to that, you used chronology-based questioning with your clients but rarely used a chronological model in your final deliverable. Sorry, *memoir*. This certainly helped us. We had to teach 'Freddie' human time. 'The Braid,' we call it. Humans really aren't linear. They're *messy*." The man called Eric actually wrinkled his nose. "Your methodology helped—your data extraction. Chronological time was easier for her to grasp initially. Simplistic time. But now—"

"Not that your work was simplistic." Marco tapped her arm. "In fact, your use of marginalia aided the model. Didn't it, Eric?"

"Quotidian Proust stuff." Eric actually offered a thumbs-up. "She's intuitive now."

They were all staring at Freddie. "I'm glad I could help. Do you need me to sign something? Is this because I need to give, um, some kind of . . ." Freddie couldn't think.

"No, Freddie," Rosemary answered. "That's all been taken care of."

Later, Freddie wondered why this didn't register. She would return to this moment repeatedly and wonder why. Ego is a powerful force.

"You said before that I was 'representative,'" Freddie began. "Flattering, kind of, but it seems a little off. Doesn't it to you? I mean, white, middle America, native English speaker, middle class, two kids . . ." Her voice grew duller by the minute. "That doesn't seem correct? Or especially useful."

"Think of it this way," Rajat said. "You could very easily be the Indian version or the Chinese version. You'd still like Madonna, you'd still feel overwhelmed at Costco, and you'd still be the kind of woman who occasionally photographs the contents of her purse. You're not special. No one is."

"Okay." *He was such a dick.*

"Let's think of it another way." Marco lifted a hand. "Freddie, people outsourced some of the most important moments of their lives to you. In real time. Others shared the most personal stories of their lives. They all let you in for a reason. You knew exactly what questions to ask. You understood what they needed, who they needed you to be, and when they needed help most."

"She's a chameleon," Rosemary said. "She can reflect anyone."

"Then, you used what they'd shared to create something for them. A product that allowed your clients to feel seen and heard. It was important for us to accomplish that aspect as well."

"So . . ." Freddie was trying to keep up. "You've created a virtual assistant that helps people make decisions and produces memoirs for them?"

"Not *memoirs*," Rajat muttered. "Think again."

"Freddie, you inspired us." Marco looked as sincere as his voice. "Now, we simply want your advice. We're showing you an early prototype—not the real deal, but still. We want to hear from you." Marco nodded towards the screen. "Enough talking. Let's introduce you. Freddie, just say your name."

Everyone grinning. "Freddie," she said.

"I am here," came the answer.

By the time the screen went dark, Freddie could barely breathe.

"I thought we agreed to show her the Diane Keaton thing. Not this one." Marco was staring at Rajat.

"The great kitchen, the ocean." Rosemary nodded. "In the last meeting . . . I thought he told you—"

Nostalgia is dangerous, Freddie almost said it out loud. She swallowed, trying to push everything back down, her throat constricting; she began to cough. Of course, they would go with that. They were banking on fear.

Marco motioned for someone to get Freddie a glass of water, but no one seemed to want to actually pour the water. Who would pour the water? Not the women—that was sexist bullshit. Not the men—it wasn't their job. Not Marco. Not Rosemary.

Freddie kept coughing and poured the water herself. The air seemed to return to the room.

"Our apologies," Marco said, after she'd taken a few sips. "We'd planned on showing you a different example. But, that being said, your thoughts?"

The room emptied of sound. Freddie took her time.

"I'm overwhelmed," she said. "It is . . ."

"Captured imagination." Rajat grinned.

"Yes." Freddie nodded slowly.

"She's stunned." Rosemary almost giggled. "That in itself. Well done, team."

Freddie's mind began to wander. They'd used that scene in her memoir as well as her Uber driver preferences. Because it was the way all warnings began—*A girl went off on her own. A girl drank one too many*. Back then, she could have been taken and become the stolen bride of a taxi driver, never to be heard from again. But that didn't happen. He'd merely taken her back to her host family's compound. He took her home. That was what happened. But "Freddie" told a different story. *She* had the ability to turn it all into an opening scene of a *Law and Order* episode. Complete with booming theme music. Freddie felt sick.

"This is just one of the more poppy functions. Like you, 'Freddie' doesn't just assist and advise, she offers a gift. Think of the daily stories people tell 'Freddie' as snapshots in a kind of photo stream. They are tools of creation. People can put themselves in their favorite shows and then upload it. Imagine what the millenials will do with *Friends*."

Freddie searched for his hat through the glass. He was still there, eating crackers and talking to Willa. Freddie wasn't paying close enough attention. *Dear God*, she thought.

"This will not only change the future politically and economically, 'Freddie' will also be a force for personal expression." Marco looked serious. "Everyone deserves a voice. Our story is incomplete unless we hear from everyone."

You're good. Freddie knew she was exhaling too loudly.

"Now that you've seen just a little of what 'Freddie' can do," Marco began, "we'd like you to answer a few questions. Give us some feedback. We used so much of the resources you helped create as an Outsourcer. We need *you*, Freddie!" Marco leaned forward. "And we'd love it if you could go with us to TED. Our big event. The stage where we reveal 'Freddie.' This is going to change everything. We will all be able to understand how to better serve our world. Especially our world in crisis."

For a minute, Freddie thought Marco might hold her hand, but instead, he held his own. "I can promise you this, Freddie. We are never going to sell out. Open source, using a Jimmy Wales Wiki-model. We'll create a foundation. 'Freddie' can be on any device—*every* device. The world will own this information. And you'll be there with us."

"Freddie is just about to begin a short leave. A family situation." Rosemary's hand held steady over the table.

"Of course, of course," Marco murmured. He passed Freddie a glossy TED folder and a sticker. The Brené Brown, Ray Kurzweil, Pico Iyer, Elizabeth Gilbert, Pranav Mistry TED!? *Holy, holy, holy shit!* How easily we humans can forget.

"I would *love* to go." Freddie held the folder. Of course, she'd like to go. Be honest, who wouldn't? TED! "But I'll have to see how everything progresses . . . with the situation Rosemary just mentioned." *They don't need to know everything* rang out in Freddie's head, clearly Mister's voice. Freddie tried to smile less pitifully. "My Dad will totally love this. Of course, I won't tell him where or how I got it. But he loves TED and T-E-D happens to be his first three initials." Three names before you even reached the hyphenate. *Stop talking!* "Believe me, I'd really love to go." Freddie placed the TED folder inside the MemCorps™ leather one.

"So you still have a relationship with them?" Kelly asked. "Your parents, I mean."

"Of course I have a relationship with them," Freddie laughed.

"It's just, you wrote about—"

"That was my twenties." Freddie knew her face was red. She didn't feel well.

"I just expected—"

"I'm afraid I need to go," Freddie said, eyes never far from the triceratops hat through the glass door. He was getting tired. It was past time.

"We'll keep in close touch," Marco said, giving Freddie's arm another squeeze. "Best of luck."

"Just a reminder," Rosemary interrupted. "Everything we've discussed in this room is confidential." Rosemary shrugged, her thin gold earrings in motion. "Spouses included."

"Rosemary told me about your upcoming leave," Willa said as they parted outside the MemCorps™ office.

Freddie nodded, getting him into the jogger. She would smile only when he looked at her. They would take the train home. He would like that and people would be there and she would not cry.

"Come on, Freddie. You're great in a crisis—" But Willa stopped. "He's a strong, lovely boy. You're strong too, by the way." It was the closest Willa had ever come to complimenting her.

"I'm not sure about that anymore," Freddie said. Her throat tight. Her boy still holding his cars, chattering away about the red convertible parked across the street.

"Here." Willa held out her hand.

Freddie looked. It was a piece of paper with a phone number written on it. Willa was breaking an Outsourcers Rule! No last name, but there on the paper—one two three-four five six-seven eight nine ten digits that identified the person she was outside of work.

We live in a slender townhouse with shared walls and a shared roof and a shared alleyway surrounded by people trying desperately to ignore each other. We live in a slender townhouse in Middlefield where the mark of a good neighbor is a signed confidentiality agreement.

"You need a walk," Mister said. "Go." He'd found her crying in the shower.

Now, nothing was the same. Nothing normal. Freddie woke when her son woke from the pain. She held him most of the day. She tried to keep her daughter's life a version of itself. *Facsimile*, Freddie thought. Freddie had to ask people for help every day. Other mothers brought her daughter home from school, often delivering a meal for that evening. Freddie didn't care about happiness or stories. Parenting and marriage are not for the faint of heart. *I need to be kinder to my own parents*, Freddie thought. *More forgiving.* It was enough that they'd made it through a day—and then a night—after the fire. How did they even go on? Freddie had to stop herself from staring at the sidewalk. She barely noticed the trees.

Freddie began to narrate her steps so she would pay attention. *You can walk year-round in California. Even in the rain. And if you notice the stars, and the sounds of the CalTrain and the VTA, and the people coming home late from work by car, on foot, lights ablaze on bicycle—you can witness this world at its most workaday normal, at its most ethereal. We, the People waiting for our grocery delivery. Our homes just alike, leaning in to our world as our shared walls last through the tremors of Life.*

She took a breath. It was that feeling you get when someone is born or dies and you walk out into the world and no one else knows, but you still must take one step after another in the knowledge of miracles. And it's just a Tuesday—Freddie almost smiled. They are just putting away their cans of soup. Freddie looked up at a lit window, knowing it was a bathroom just like her own. The shampoo bottles dark in the backlight.

How could anyone explain to a three-year-old that the pain would go away? There was no yesterday or tomorrow or that moment in the future. Some children forget afterwards. Freddie understood this. She had no memories before the fire. And then, her little brother was born and her parents—*Joan*—began again to breathe. It was as if an announcement had been made—*we can all finally start living again*. And so they did, and Freddie began to create memory.

Can the absence of pain alone be joy? *Please.* She wiped her nose on her sleeve. *Please let him have that, and more.* The risks post-surgery were many. He'd had an infection before. Hip surgery was a constant threat. Keep him still; keep him whole. Freddie always pointed to the posters kept in the specialist's hallway of Mia Hamm and Troy Aikman, Kristi Yamaguchi and David Lynch. Never would she point to a picture of Lord Byron. Never did they mention the generations who came before her little boy, the others her son would never meet. *Genetics . . . keep him whole. Him . . . and her.* When her daughter came home, Freddie just tried to be as Normal as she could.

Normal. The last time Freddie had been outside was the post-op appointment. They were told to fill yet another new prescription. Her husband and son waiting in the car as she hurried inside the CVS; the pain set to restart in thirty minutes.

"We don't carry that," the pharmacist said. She was already thinking about groceries they needed. *Hurry, please.* She had thirty minutes, twenty-nine, twenty-eight. Reminding herself of their luck; all she had to do was show the card and the pills would be cheaper than some lattes. It was unfair. They were too lucky. Then, she heard the pharmacist say something. *No, it couldn't be.*

"I'm sorry, can you please spell the prescription for me?" Freddie asked. She wasn't being racist exactly. She was tired. She never heard well.

He spelled it slowly: "C-i-p-r-o."

The pharmacist didn't know the story. *If he'd read my memoir he'd know what that word means to me*, Freddie thought, almost laughing. She wished she could download it to him instantly. Could "Freddie" do that? What if stories—*intelligence*—could actually lead to direct action? That was it, really; that was Marco Villatoni's gift to the world. *Welcome to Stories*, Freddie had the urge to impersonate. *Make it funny. You need funny.*

"Just one moment please." She didn't even say thank you. She should have. The pharmacist was trying to help. Did he know she was running out of time?

She walked out to the driver's side of their car. Mister rolled down the window. "The script is for Cipro, not Septra." She was using the hospital talk, the way she and Mister spoke to each other in these times. "We need to call the doc back. The pharmacy here doesn't carry it. It will take days to get. I'm highly allergic to Cipro. I mean *highly*." Her husband, of all people, should know this. Why did she even have to explain this?

He hadn't read it. He lived with her, wasn't that enough? She'd never asked him to read it. Why would he? Had they once been people squeezing themselves into a single bed with the shades drawn for days, telling each other the stories of their lives? It's only how you begin. It's not how you live.

And that's when Freddie saw the tree in Middlefield. On the corner, just before the townhouse with the Halloween decorations up year-round. No children lived in the house, just three adults of odd ages. Housemates probably. But there, on the tree in front of their townhome, the limbs held out glasses on one branch and a sari scarf on another.

I love this place, Freddie thought. *I just want it to love me back. I want it to see me and say: Live here forever.* And this tree was proof enough for Freddie. It was a sign. This time, unlike the other surgeries before, Freddie told people. She had to. "We can't do everything ourselves," she'd said to Mister. "I agree that we don't want him to be defined by it, but at the same time, we can't keep everything hidden. It makes it feel wrong. And, sometimes too, you just need help."

There was joy. We will help each other.

It was the neighbors, the school friends, Maribel, and the Marias who had helped. It wasn't The Company or any of Mister's colleagues. To be fair, Freddie hadn't heard a word from the other Outsourcers or any of her clients either. *At least Willa had tried*, Freddie thought.

We live in a slender townhouse between.

"Our temporary world," Freddie said quietly to herself as if there were no other. "We leave breadcrumbs in the trees." *Here is your sari scarf. Here are your glasses. Please don't leave me behind. Again. Don't leave me.*

She said hello. She recognized them. They must have moved into that place on Gladys. She'd seen them in a white Prius. She'd smiled at them before, nodded while pushing the stroller to school pick-up. She'd seen them as the kids raced on their scooters.

"Excuse me," the woman said. Freddie turned, smiling. She had decided to stop worrying. She should be grateful. *It's the end of the world as we know it and he would be fine.* Ohm. Shanti. Breathe. Gratitude. She'd do anything to keep him whole. Be anyone. The bartering would begin again when he woke at 2:00 a.m. sweating, screaming, but now she could take the time to smile at her neighbors. *I'm exhausted, but so are they. We take care of each other.*

But the couple pulled out identification. They were under the streetlight. Freddie could see well enough to read that these people weren't neighbors or even, possibly, a couple. They were federal agents.

"Could we have a few minutes of your time, Freddie?"

six

The townhouse was seemingly identical to Freddie's rental, but this one was nicer. No carpeting. The Feds got wood flooring. A trestle table, some chairs, and an actual painting on the wall, even if it was a faux Kandinsky. No horrible blinds. *They got the wooden shutters*, Freddie thought as she walked inside between the agents, *but their kitchen light probably buzzed too*.

Freddie wondered, idiotically, if the agents also had to turn off their heating to fill up the hot water tank enough to have showers. Luckily, Middlefield was built in California, otherwise an inconvenient truth could get pretty chilly. It was Freddie's job to turn the heat off (or turn it on) at the correct times in the winter. Jobs such as these fall to people who don't sleep. People at home. Freddie even considered, just for a moment, about walking up the agents' stairs and looking at the rooms. They wouldn't sleep here, would they?

"You've written a lot in the last year, haven't you, Freddie?" the female agent began.

"Is this about my Wikipedia use?" Freddie asked.

It was too easy, too difficult *not* to keep some whiff of Wikipedia in the writing. With so many clients and so many stories set in places she had to imagine, Freddie had researched more in the last year than she could possibly remember. And not just geography, but also the history of the places she needed to write around a client. Details. Setting was crucial in a memoir-for-hire. Freddie would bring up Jane Goodall if she had to. Another childhood idol. *We're all human*, Freddie thought, *even dear Jane.*

"It has come to our knowledge that you have been contacted by a group."

The male agent had her memoir on his laptop and flicked through a few pages on-screen in Freddie's full view. It was odd to see. Words she no longer recognized as her own. They read like someone else's. It was all so long ago.

"A *company?*"—the female agent sounded doubtful—"called Mem-Corps?" No trademark necessary.

"It's odd, kind of." The male agent was at the scene in Kuzgen where Freddie was teaching at the University. "You don't seem like the same person?"

"You should take it all with a grain of salt," Freddie said. She was suddenly exhausted. Too much adrenaline. She never had the proper responses at the proper times. "I wrote it awhile ago. To be honest, I can't even remember that well now. I mean, the original experience of it." She made a sound, a rueful kind of noise. "Actually, the truth is, I wrote it in a month. Ridiculous, to say the least. I have no idea now what made it in there and what didn't."

"Terrorists," the male agent said. "You wrote about your relationship with terrorists."

"Not really." Freddie was freezing cold. Not just her hands and her feet. *I'm tired*, she thought. "They were wonderful people. They took me into their homes."

"We would like to redefine your concept of terrorist." The female agent nodded.

Freddie, you wrote a memoir about a place where, after you left, the American government landed planes, opened up a military base, and—if you believe the Internet—waterboarded known terrorists in a black-ops facility just outside the capital.

"I want to go home."

Both agents nodded, but no one got up from the table. They were both ridiculously good-looking. *This is almost like a movie*, Freddie thought. *A super fit, expensively dressed African-American couple in Silicon Valley. You should run this fucking place! Black and female is rare here; hell, black and male is rare. Move in for real! You belong here more than I do.*

"You're my neighbors, but you're not." Freddie felt lightheaded. "And you're real. You're real agents. In Middlefield, and I've already forgotten your names."

"Agent Kent," he said, pointing towards the female agent. "Agent Richards." He placed a hand on his chest.

"We have reason to believe that several corporations and even a few governments have targeted you in your connection with MemCorps." Agent Kent held out a file. A real, actual file with paperwork and photos: dates and times, locations and names. "Let me be clear, they've targeted you and your family."

"What?" Freddie was now more than awake. "Listen, I don't know what you're talking about. I wrote an ebook, not even a real book . . ."

"You understand more people can read ebooks now, Freddie? Way more accessible than hardcover."

"I never thought about it that way," Freddie answered.

"You don't deny that you work for a firm called The Outsourcers?"

Agent Kent interrupted. "You might not know this, but some of the people you've been working with have ties to the hacker group Anonymous, as well as certain elements in Russia, Pakistan, the Middle East, and North Korea, just to name a few. Big Data means Big Money."

"We also have reason to believe that another organization called TOTO is also tracking you," Agent Richards said.

Freddie let out a hysterical giggle. "Sorry."

"It stands for *Turn Off, Tune Out*. They are an environmental group with a radical agenda. Targeting data centers and tech hubs. Opposed to energy waste. Big on privacy rights and vindicating human rights abuses by the tech giants. 'Change by any means necessary.'" His fingers provided air quotes. "It isn't a joke, I promise you."

"No," Freddie gulped. "Of course it isn't." *This is the world we live in*, she thought. *This* is the world we live in. "Timothy Leary."

"Excuse me?" Agent Richards was still gliding past the pages of Freddie's ebook.

"Turn on, tune in, drop out. They just switched it around." Freddie was sick of remembering. This was about *her* family. No one was going to target her family, especially on her account. Freddie had never been so scared in her life. "What can I do?"

"Unlike some people, we don't use the term 'terrorist' lightly, Ms. Flint-Smythe." Agent Kent opened another file and began pulling out numerous surveillance photos. Freddie and Ben at ChronosCoffee. Freddie walking into HackerSpace. Freddie driving her Volvo, her mouth open wide, screaming, her kids in the back. Wait a minute. No, she wasn't screaming. They were singing.

"I'm not a terrorist," Freddie said. She tried to stop herself from narrating, from moving away from the actual moment.

"Freddie, MemCorps will go live," Agent Richards said, handing her a glass of water.

"It's not mine." Freddie knew she was almost shouting.

"We know." Agent Kent looked as if she wanted to smack her.

"Put it this way—you'd make changes at this point, perhaps," Agent Richards prompted, "to '*Freddie*?'"

"Maybe," Freddie said. "I don't know."

Both agents gave her a look.

"Excuse us for a minute." The female agent nodded.

I need to remember, Freddie thought. Both agents were standing on the other side of the living room, under the windows that you couldn't open even if you wanted to.

What should she say? *Does an NDA even count when being questioned by federal agents?* "I'm just a little concerned," Freddie began. Both agents turned to look at her. "I mean, I only saw the prototype, but it was a lot."

Agent Richards shook his head. "Freddie, MemCorps is a good thing."

"A *very* good thing." Agent Kent gave her the smallest smile in the world. *Too beautiful*, Freddie thought. *Bad casting. They should have sent ugly agents. I'm sitting in an Elmore Leonard novel . . . Focus, Freddie.*

"But what do you want me to do?"

"Nothing really." Agent Kent shrugged. "But, now that you're asking, we believe you've found yourself in the middle of a mess. You are, in some ways, the worst kind of civilian. You figure a certain amount out through a kind of intuition, I'm guessing here. And, based on that, you make a mess without understanding the . . . uh . . . ramifications."

"A mess," Freddie repeated. "Let me get this straight. I've made a mess and you don't want me to fix it?"

Agent Kent nodded. "The people you've been colluding with, they're easily manipulated."

"I'm not *colluding* with anyone."

"Freddie, you seem to trust the wrong people." Agent Kent pushed her chair in and got her own glass of water. "Naïve. Bad instincts." They were finished.

"I have bad instincts?" Freddie wasn't finished. How could she stand and protect her family and make this right if she couldn't even trust herself?

"Freddie, what you've helped create is important because it provides an on-going backstory. That is all we can say in explanation. From this point on, no one will be without a story. The right to be forgotten no longer an option. We want to keep that intact. Your country is grateful. Our concern was based on your possible actions."

"*Re*actions," Agent Kent muttered.

"I don't understand."

"'Freddie' is a game changer," Agent Richards explained. "Certain factions,"—Freddie rattled off the list in her head of the countries, states, organizations, and corporations that might be included—"well, they're interested. That's all you need to know. You, personally, need to do nothing."

"Nothing," Agent Kent repeated.

Both agents stared at Freddie as if expecting her to say something. Freddie had no idea what. Minutes passed. Agent Richards got a call and left the room. Agent Kent ignored Freddie and sat back down as she read from her screen.

I should have known they weren't my real neighbors, Freddie thought. *Damn it. I should have known. Dear Federal Bureau of Investigation, in future, make pretend Silicon Valley "neighbors" a mixed-race couple. He's a Sikh from Berlin, she's from Connecticut, the grandparents are Chinese-German from Toronto. A gay couple.* Freddie imagined them all having a picnic on the green. The agents had children too, of course, in Freddie's mind. You almost have to in Middlefield.

Agent Kent looked up from her screen. "Freddie, if something should come your way—do not follow it."

"I'm not sure I understand." Freddie's head ached.

"You'll understand if and when it happens. Don't try to fix this." Her voice was firm.

"Okay." Freddie had no idea what else to say.

"Your instincts could get you into a mess of trouble."

Gee, thanks, Freddie kept herself from saying, but she accidentally waved when she turned to leave. It was an involuntary reaction to exiting a Middlefield townhouse. And, still, Freddie nearly apologized. Agent Kent just nodded and shut the door.

Of course, they weren't really married, Freddie thought. She almost tripped in the dark. Agent Richards held her arm down the final three steps. He seemed to be walking to his car but also alongside her.

"Aren't you supposed to give me a business card?" Freddie asked. "In case I need to be in touch."

"No," Agent Richards said, smiling. "We're just letting you know to be on your guard. You aren't currently under investigation. We don't want you to do a thing," he said, quietly, and then his voice shifted. "Don't worry, Freddie. A friendly heads-up."

"I thought you were my neighbors," Freddie whispered. "People move around a lot here. They come and go."

"Sorry to disappoint you," he said, standing alongside the Prius. "It's a nice neighborhood, Freddie. You're lucky to have found it."

"It is," Freddie said, a little out of breath. "I am."

"Your hands are bad tonight," Mister said when Freddie came in, his eyes on her glass. "You need to call the doctor."

"We've seen enough doctors." She didn't mean to sound that way. This wasn't his fault. No matter how she looked at it, it couldn't be his fault. How does one even begin to explain? *You know that walk I just took . . .*

Freddie saw herself bending down at the foot of the bed. *See Freddie on bended knee, in need of mercy.* She'd betrayed him—*them*—she'd done exactly what he hated. She'd shared a piece of herself with everyone. She hadn't kept everything for *them*. She did this. Freddie.

I've broken our marriage vows. I've told too much.

Freddie thought of ego. She thought of federal informants. She thought of Kim Dot Com and Assange and Cumberbatch and informants in drag and Snowden hugging the flag. She thought of every bit of the conversation she'd just had and every version and every outcome. Finally, she pictured herself being waterboarded in the upstairs bathroom of the agents' townhome, the one identical to the one she bathed her kids in. But the Feds wouldn't have a shower curtain.

"I walked," she said instead, knowing that this was despair.

Her phone buzzed. A text from Ben: *Now that Outscrers closed will you still work for me? Justwonderin ;)* She texted back: *What?*

"Do you feel better?" her husband asked over the screen resting on his legs. He would have tracked her. That's why he always had her take her phone. There she would be on a map, in their neighborhood. Even if he'd checked just a few minutes ago, he wouldn't think anything of it. She was still in the neighborhood, her dot glowing.

Her phone beeped: *Chk email.*

Ben forwarded the email he'd been sent: *Thank you for being a preferred client of The Outsourcers. We have loved assisting you. Due to our recent acquisition, we have closed our Cupertino office. Please know that your loyalty has been . . .*

Freddie stopped and started the email again. She looked through her account, her voicemail. She pressed *The O* in her contact list. The number was disconnected. She ran downstairs, opened up her purse, and remembered. Freddie closed the downstairs blinds. It was here, she knew it. In the pocket of her kid bag. She found the paper. Dialed the number. It rang once and went to voicemail. Not Willa's voice. An automaton. Freddie left a message.

Freddie looked. The lights were now off at the townhome she'd just been in, all the windows in the alley shuttered. All, except for one. She'd seen it. There, just now. The neighbor with the Lotus. Two circles peering out. Circles against glass.

In the morning, Freddie saw that the circles were actually two owl-shaped window prisms. Mister and their girl left for work and school, and Freddie put *Bedknobs and Broomsticks* on and forwarded to the scene where the generations of knights and soldiers come to life on the hill.

"They're just costumes," her son explained again on the couch. He was doing better today. Much better. "Not real knights. Mrs. Price helps them. It's magic."

"Yes," Freddie said. She propped him up higher and moved away, the

59

pillows taking the place her body left behind.

It was his favorite part. She might let him watch it twice this morning. Maybe even three times. Freddie poured herself another cup of coffee and looked out into the alley. She felt raw, yet hyperaware. It was quiet, all the windows shuttered, everyone gone to work and school. Then, her neighbor's garage door went up, and their gold Prius reversed slowly out. Of course, it was Hansa's first day back at Google. Her maternity leave now over. Freddie remembered dropping those gifts off, that bag of stuff. She and Hansa had emailed back and forth between their shared wall the day before yesterday. *We're in for a transition*, Hansa wrote. *Do you ever stop wishing you were always someplace else? How are things for all of you? I'm glad you liked the soup and baguette. You didn't need to send me a thank you note! I just wish I could do more. Time has become the enemy.*

Freddie picked up her phone and tried The Outsourcers again (disconnected). She left another message for Willa. She didn't have a number for the agents. Freddie even tried the phone number she had for Mem-Corps. She felt sick listening to the ring. Marco Villatoni was not an evil man. Hell, he worked for NPR for decades. Maybe he didn't fully realize the power of what they'd created. It sounded like a movie. It was laughable, except it wasn't. Big Data. That's what the agents kept referencing. What Rajat/Surya spewed: *We're humanizing Big Data. We're creating an Age of Empathy.*

Freddie knew enough about Big Data. Her Mister was a specialist at keeping Big Data alive. Accessible. Always on. Backed up. Freddie thought of "Freddie." *I am now Big Data.* Freddie felt sick. Nothing seemed real. She pressed the numbers again. The MemCorps office voicemail system was at least in place. But no one was in the office yet. It was too early in Silicon Valley. People were still working out or running errands. Riding overpriced road bikes up to Alice's for breakfast and back before the first meeting. Life didn't start until closer to 10:00 a.m. *Please press one at any time.* Freddie would try again later. She tossed her phone roughly on the counter only to pick it up again and press a name. "Hi Mom," Freddie said into the phone.

She waited, listening to her mother's voice. The words less important than the sound itself.

"Well . . ." Freddie answered her mother's question slowly. "The medicine seems to be working. No, he's watching that part on the hill with the Nazis."

"They aren't Nazis," the boy bellowed. "They're retired soldiers. Soldiers of the Old Home Guard."

"We need to go over that again," Freddie heard herself saying. "Anyway, he's doing a lot better. It's going to be a better day." Freddie felt weak. "Tell me how you all are."

"It's been eventful here," Joan began. That's how Joan always started, but then she told a long story with settings ranging from doctors' offices to care centers to hospitals with multiple names. And it all came down to one sentence. "Your Gram has been diagnosed with Alzheimer's. A fast-acting Alzheimer's, actually."

It sounded like a cleaning product to Freddie. She saw the commercial in her mind, the box, the label: *You too can have fast-acting Alzheimer's!* Horrible. She was horrible to even think it. She couldn't help herself. *Wipes away memory in just one . . .*

Joan was still talking.

"Can I call her?" Freddie asked.

"Give her time to get settled. You understand the implications, Freddie. We'll have to sell her house, her car—"

"Mom, I'm so sorry."

"Your Gram hasn't been herself in so long. It's horrible. Sometimes it feels like I'm forgetting the person she was, but I've been here the whole time."

And I haven't, Freddie thought.

Freddie felt guilty. She opened up the travel websites while she listened. It was while filling out the dates, the first *available* dates that were not a piano recital weekend or any of his physical therapy, that Freddie realized why those numbers meant anything. An ad appeared—new books out from Gilbert, Brown, and Kurzweil. Of course, it was the same weekend as TED.

The sight of the embossed leather MemCorps™ made her dizzy. The TED brochure filled with pictures of anyone who was doing anything of "value." Freddie told herself that it had all been in service to something useful. *Valuable!* Even according to the agents, The Outsourcers hadn't really been *illusion-for-hire*. Sometimes, instead of making someone appear *perfect*, Freddie had seen the truth and reflected that back. She was just about to reach a connection of threads, but her mind fluttered back.

Freddie saw it. There in the TED file was an airline ticket. *A sign.* She looked up the specifics while Joan was talking about treatments. Freddie just had to pay a fee to change her destination. *See*, Freddie told herself, *everything works out the way it's supposed to.* One ticket to Indiana for a weekend so she could help. So Freddie could say goodbye.

"That's the perfect time." Joan sounded as if she were talking to a stranger. "Your father's retirement party is that weekend."

Freddie listened to her mother as the last scene of the movie played on the screen, as the Home Guard soldiers were marching away and the children thought, for just a moment, that their adventures were over. They looked so disappointed.

It was later that morning, after Freddie hung up the phone. After other doses of medicine, other loads of laundry and stacks of Golden Books read aloud; after repeating to herself: *I don't want to forget.*

Why is it, as humans, when someone is in crisis, we put ourselves in their shoes? We practice, in a way, for their life. For what *could* happen to us. Of course, Freddie began to think she would also get Alzheimer's—*I'm going to someday forget myself.*

Freddie typed in the search term: *Freddie MemCorps.* Nothing. No results that linked the two terms together.

Freddie tried to access her memoir, her ebook, *The Roof of Life.* It was nowhere. No longer available. No longer in existence. She was now a 404.

Freddie kept searching. She started with her first name. The most popular result being:

Frederica ("Freddie") von Duran Hatton-Heath

From Wikipedia, the free encyclopedia

Dame **Fredericka ("Freddie") Veronique Marie von Duran Hatton-Heath** (**Mrs Henry James Selvedge**), DBE[1] (born 14 April 1893 in Paris, France; died 17 April 1933 in Siena, Italy) was a British explorer and travel writer. She wrote more than two dozen books on her travels in the Middle East, Africa, and Afghanistan, as well as several autobiographic works and essays. A famed cartographer, the maps she made of the Serengeti region of Africa are still in use today.

Contents [hide]
1 Early life and studies
2 Travels and writings
3 Writings
4 See also
5 References
6 Sources and further reading
7 External links

"We're back to the beginning," Freddie said.

"Mama," her son called. "Soup?"

"Of course," Freddie replied. "*Please. Please*, may I have soup?"

For about an hour, Freddie thought it might be a fluke. (In a singsong voice: *Accidents Happen.*) Between stirring, pouring, assisting, tidying, washing the same load of laundry twice, she kept checking. But then, after lunch, the mail arrived, and Freddie got the letter. Rosemary Rafferty no longer wrote using The Outsourcers letterhead. This was from MemCorps™. Official. Freddie's book was no longer even an ebook. It was now, simply, a piece—*"an integral part"*—of MemCorps™.

"You're collecting lives?" she'd asked Marco at the meeting. No wonder the agents in their almost townhouse, across and to the right of her own, loved "Freddie." They would somehow use "Freddie" to monitor everyone. They'd be able to look into her home and watch Freddie and her family playing the parts of their lives in cross-section. *There she goes up the stairs with the laundry again.* But "Freddie" allowed for even more access, a deeper kind of truth or lie. *The stories we tell ourselves. You can't be complacent with "Freddie." You hit all our search terms.*

"Freddie" wasn't her. But that was the promise? Her, but better. Every person she could be. Every search term she could inhabit even for just a moment or a decade or a week. She watched out the window as her neighbor pulled their gold Prius back in, so silently, probably returning with pumped breast milk, checking in. Mother. Wife. Daughter. Employer. Employee. Food. Ponytail. Home. Work.

"Freddie" can handle everything.

Freddie finally understood: "I've been replaced."

Freddie walked her son into town an hour before they had to pickup the girl. His leg elevated as she pushed the stroller up the two hills to Castro. She kept up the conversation about knights. He was doing better. Another few weeks and he'd almost be back. *How do people live like this?* Freddie thought. *In this? We just do it for two months at a time, maybe three with the physical therapy; four if you counted the worry. Sure, we seem to go through it every year, but still.* How do people live inside of this for decades, for a lifetime? How had her parents survived after the fire? *I just need to get us back to Normal.* What would "Freddie" do right now? Were *choices* even available? *No choice or too many*—was that it? Can you really live in the in-between?

Make a choice.

"We're getting gelato," Freddie announced. "We need a treat." She would stop by the MemCorps™ office, she would ask some questions, everything would be fine. But that didn't happen. Castro Street was still the same—Chinese herbalists, fake Irish pub, hipster hot dog place, Korean, Pho, Indian, sushi, noodles, and gelato. But MemCorps™ no longer existed. Freddie tried the door, she rang the bell; she even crossed the street for a better view. The door was locked. The lights were off. The blinds up. No monitor in sight.

The painted letters were gone. Brown paper covered the window, but on her tiptoes, Freddie could see through a tear. The office was empty. No more minimalist acacia, Willa's tower of a desk was gone. Almost certainly no plush Rosemary office or Round Table lunchroom; nothing left. It was as if The Outsourcers never existed. Soo-Jin. Carl. Belinda. Jamila. She didn't know their last names. Freddie thought about how it was when they'd eaten together. How they shared clients. How they told their stories.

Soo-Jin had a client, one of the original Yahoo surfers who arrived well before the first bubble. Born in Iowa of German-Scotch descent, this woman adopted a baby girl from China as a single parent. The baby was now a preteen, and they lived in Cupertino. The mother, "Sun Tea," cried during her first meeting with Soo-Jin, saying, "I need you, Soo-Jin. I do everything wrong! Too many ham salad sandwiches, too much sun tea." (That's how she got her name.) And so Soo-Jin called Freddie: "You need to come translate Sun Tea."

"What is this place?" Freddie's daughter asked.

"It's where I used to work when you were at school," Freddie said. She wondered where Soo-Jin was at that moment. Freddie fantasized about riding to Sun Tea's house and happening upon Soo-Jin. *We were just in the neighborhood.* But Soo-Jin wouldn't be at Sun Tea's. Soo-Jin knew better. Maybe she'd be at Sprouts? Freddie could see it. The two of them carrying their bags.

Do nothing, the agents said. Freddie knew if she contacted any client of any Outsourcers Associate she'd be sued. They would take everything. They—Rosemary—MemCorps. Marco Villatoni may have promised open source in the name of Linus Torvalds, but where did that leave Freddie?

"Firsty!" her son shouted. "Now!" He was repairing *and* regressing. Just like last time.

"Me too," Freddie's daughter agreed. "But we need to clean our hands."

What have I done? Freddie thought, looking at her daughter. She'd messed them up already. They would blame her too, someday, soon.

She remembered watching Sun Tea nod at everything Soo-Jin said. She remembered the wallpaper and the yellow coffee mugs hanging in the kitchen. She remembered the rosebushes and succulents in the front. Freddie knew she could find it again. She turned to where her children were pointing. Kanteens forgotten in hand, mouths open like puppies, her children stared at the white letters on the green awning, a word they would always remember: "Starbucks!"

Freddie rang the doorbell of the agents' townhouse. Her daughter helping herself to a realtor flier, asking questions, expecting answers. Her son brandishing two twigs, pretending his pockets were holsters, all while singing, "We don't believe in G-U-N-S!"

The sign outside read: FOR SALE, OPEN HOUSE, SAT and SUN. When they'd moved to California, this townhouse was worth about

$550,000. Now the flier outside listed the asking price as $1,205,000. And the owners would get more, not less. Much, much more. Alien cars would kluge this street on Saturday. Sports cars belonging to the newly married, the child-free. No neighbor would be able to park in their normal spot until nightfall. People would offer in cash plus a hundred thousand extra, a rumored buy-up of Silicon Valley properties by a Chinese syndicate. The townhouse would be sold by Sunday.

The agents were gone.

They were in bed.

"Do you ever feel like you're just a mouse in a maze?" Freddie was trying not to cry. She couldn't tell him everything and that felt like she couldn't tell him anything. "Do you ever feel like that? Like you're part of some experiment? Like maybe we all are?"

"We have choices. Even mice have choices."

They were in bed.

The four of them. Too early. Parents exhausted, drowsy with tequila.

"Why don't we watch *Swiss Family Robinson*?" Freddie suggested.

"Not again," her daughter sighed.

"No!" Her son hid his face.

"Why do you always pick that?" her daughter asked. "Do you want to live in a treehouse on an island?"

"With pirates?" her son added.

"Yes," Freddie answered.

They were in bed.

"All information is not good information. Is it?" Freddie asked. Everything felt confused. Out of order. Out of sync.

"It depends," he answered. "Information is only as good as its source."

"But in this case, the source is human." She remembered everything in that minute. Saw herself in different beds, on a floor, on a bus, riding in a car past fields of sunflowers, her feet on the dashboard, music loud, windows open, the ground shaking, the phone ringing, on a bed, sobbing. "We are human. We change constantly."

"Then the source might be an issue."

They were in bed.
"Can we talk?"
He pretended sleep. He didn't need another of her lectures.

They were in bed. He got paged.

They were in bed.
"Sometimes it feels like, since we moved here, that I have to prove myself to you. My *value*. You think that Hansa next door or Rebecca at work have more value because of how they spend their days, don't you? They are more valuable than I am."

When no quick response arrived, she almost felt sorry for him. "Fuck you."

"Someone has to pay the bills, Freddie," he began.

"I would love to make the same amount as you."

"You live in a dream world." He pushed himself up on his pillows. "Trust me. I know you work hard. You do everything for us. It's just here—"

She let him talk. Divorce fantasies blossomed. Entire weekends to herself. She would read all night. Mainline entire seasons. Take dance lessons and hiking trips. Never cook. But—she would have to make a resume.

"Do you even like me anymore?" *Everyone goes through this*.

"I married you."

"Did you like me better then?"

When he didn't answer, when he began so obviously considering the question—

They were in bed.
There is a choice here somewhere, Freddie knew. She looked up at the ceiling, at the corners of the room in case spiders were cameras.

"Not a lot of options," he sighed, remote already in hand. "What do you want?"

"Comedy or action," she answered, still staring at the corners. No more mouse. No more maze. She'd think about her options later. "Want some sex?"

They were in bed. Freddie couldn't get back to sleep. The sprinklers were on outside. She couldn't remember the last time it rained. Freddie missed thunderstorms. She listened to the water. *Even our rain is virtual.*
Do nothing, Freddie. Do Not Keep My Attention. She felt desperate. It was as if life had stopped, shifted. Nothing seemed to exist from just a month before.
Do nothing.
Freddie hadn't called anyone after 8:00 p.m. in a long time. She walked all the way down to the basement, their garage. The lowest level. *I'm desperate*, she thought. Freddie called Willa's number. Again leaving a message, first whispering and then in her normal voice. She knew she sounded like an idiot.
Freddie looked at the notepad on her washing machine. She'd begun tracking how many messages she'd left Willa. Dash, dash, dash, dash, cross. Dash, dash, dash. Freddie added another dash.
It's not too late. And then Freddie thought of something she could have done weeks ago.
Freddie found an address online for a Willa Smoot in Mountain View. *Willa Smoot?* No? Yes, that was her; Freddie could see it now. The name accounted for her anger. Her rounded shoulders. Freddie looked at the clock. It was too late now, almost midnight. She would have to wait for morning.

Willa lived in a valley within a valley, not only between mountains, but also between campuses whose tallest buildings were visible in every direction. This was because Willa Smoot's neighborhood was low to the ground. It hugged the land it was parked on. Willa lived in an ordered maze of mobile homes. *New Frontier*, the sign read above a plain of concrete between the campuses.
Freddie's bike flew over three speed bumps, the empty kid chariot hopping an echo. Freddie couldn't find the right road, so she turned left, past a small section of community garden plots and a lap pool, the laundry facility, and a one-room gym with elliptical equipment. *I want to live*

here, Freddie thought. You own your home but not the land it rests on. A slower, more socialist concept. She'd never be able to talk Mister into it so that made Freddie more enthusiastic.

She was already visualizing the children here, riding their bikes beside her, when she saw Willa's car, a dented blue Mazda Miata. The tiny porch held a few tomato plants, some potted succulents, one chair, and a stool empty only for a clean ashtray. *Willa smoked?*

Freddie saw Willa through the window before she knocked. Willa sitting at a small kitchen table reading the newspaper, drinking iced tea. She was nearly close enough to touch. Willa looked up at Freddie just before she knocked. She sat there for a minute, watching Freddie, the breeze moving the newspaper. Finally, she stood and opened the door.

"Come in then." Willa's living area was lined in bookshelves. One comfortable chair and a tiny sofa. Freddie recognized the sofa. They had it as well. The smallest foldout couch IKEA made. Freddie followed Willa the two steps into the kitchen.

"So, we're out of a job." Freddie had rehearsed this line.

"Did you read your contract, Freddie?" Willa pulled an extra glass from the cupboard.

"Yes." It was almost a lie. She'd read some of it. Most of it. "It's just—I'd like to talk to Rosemary. I have a few questions."

"Rosemary is unavailable. You may direct your questions to me." How many times had Freddie heard Willa say this exact phrase into her headset?

"Willa, I'm concerned this all might be based on an incomplete—"

"What do you even want?" Willa asked.

"Something is missing." What Freddie wanted to say included federal agents. It was idiotic, really. The idea of saying she was unsure who the "bad guys" were. Perhaps even worse, she didn't want to admit that life itself felt off. Willa was watching her.

"Soon MemCorps will belong to"—Willa took a sip—"another entity. This was almost certainly in the exit statement that came with your final check."

"Okay," Freddie began cautiously. *Maybe that was in your statement, Willa! So, MemCorps was being sold!* "It just feels—" Freddie couldn't think of the word she wanted. A descriptor, a way to describe how she felt?

Erased? Betrayed? Lost? Dumped?

"Freddie, you're out of the picture. Sure, you have a talent for making people feel like their lives, their stories, are the most important in the world. You see people and they like being seen. But then, you drop them and move on to the next one." Willa laughed. "This is going to be okay. You're just not used to being on the other side. It's time to move on."

"I just thought if I could talk to Rosemary . . ."

"Freddie, the job is done. Move on." Willa finished the tea in her glass, crunching the ice.

"What if I can't?"

"Do you have a choice?"

It felt to Freddie like something shifted, like she had control over nothing and no amount of Pema Chodron or carbs or prayer or patience would ever fix this. Like something was lost. She was being tested. *And I can't save anyone*, Freddie wanted to scream. *I can't even save myself*. Freddie heard herself saying, "Just so many lives."

Willa nodded. She didn't look at Freddie. Didn't pat her on the back or the head or hug her. She sniffed. "It *is* about the collective. This was never about you. Why not focus on your family?" And then Willa started laughing. She laughed hard, her eyes crinkling. She had to wipe them with her sleeve. "The look on your face. The look on your face most of the time." She pulled a tissue out of her sleeve, blowing her nose loudly, still smiling.

"You don't know me."

Freddie stared at the refrigerator, at the pictures beneath magnets. There was one of a much younger Willa and a younger, much less polished Rosemary. They were holding beers, sitting on a picnic blanket. It looked like they were at a concert. Freddie knew nearly identical pictures existed of her. Girls leaning against each other, looking carefree. Their arms entwined.

"Freddie, you're a mess. Look at your hands. You use so much of that hand stuff, you've ruined your skin." Willa looked sad. "You can barely hear me, am I right? Earphones. Your self-protected little bubble that you think keeps you sane."

And then, as if afraid she'd said something kind, Willa barked, "Welcome to the Valley. Praying for an apocalypse or aliens, anything to keep you from having to really make your way in this world." She stood. "Listen, you found your way in. My dear, you can find your way out." Willa picked up Freddie's glass of iced tea and threw the contents in the sink. She didn't even turn around.

seven

"I can't express how good it is to see you." Freddie sat across from Ben at their old table at ChronosCoffee on a Monday after drop-off. She knew she was in violation of her NDA, her CDA, and her PIA, but she didn't care anymore. *This could almost be accidental*, she thought. She wasn't doing anything wrong. She was meeting someone for coffee. But even Freddie knew she would lie if she had to. Ben could help her. Ben *would* help her. She would fix this.

"Let's say I have a problem," she began. She didn't tell him the whole story. Somehow, she didn't have to. Ben understood.

"You know this is my kind of shit," Ben said, smiling. "I'll be honest, though. I'm surprised you didn't ask your husband."

"What are you talking about?" Freddie had just been laughing. She'd been overjoyed to see Ben, as if Ben was proof of her very existence. Ben was the only one who'd even tried, who didn't care if they got sued. Ben called her! There was no one else, not Pam or any of her other clients or Soo-Jin or Belinda. Just Ben.

"You're not supposed to know anything about me," Freddie said, her voice somehow angrier than she was. "How do you know about my husband?"

"Listen, I'm sorry. I looked at your book once, your *Middlemarch*, when you stepped away. I saw your name on the first page. Your *whole* name." He lifted his hands. "I'm sorry, Freddie. I couldn't help it. I looked you up."

He watched her trying to make decisions. Her lower lip raw.

"Listen, I'm sorry. I was just curious. Come on, you know so much about me." He waited, watching her. "Freddie, you know me. Let me help."

"Okay," she heard herself say.

"Your husband does the cloud architecture for The Company." Ben stirred his coffee. He drank it out of a metal mug with a handle that looked like it should be at a campsite instead of at a coffee place between corporate campuses in Silicon Valley. "The thing is, The Company bought MemCorps. Mergers are the fucking future, Freddie. The Company owns it all now. They wanted their own virtual assistant—their own bot. Now they have it. And 'Freddie' is going to beat Siri's ass."

Freddie felt sick. "They kept the name?"

"Of course. Gender fluid—hell ya. Your husband does their BD, uh, Big Data." Ben was on a mansplaining roll. But, for once, the tone didn't bother Freddie. She was too shocked to be bothered. "I'm just surprised you're asking for my help." Ben blushed. "Don't get me wrong; I'm thrilled. But he'd have all the access you need."

"They're going to use my work to sell stuff to people," Freddie muttered.

"They're going to use your work to sell stuff to people." Ben nodded. "And get people elected. And create more personalized media. And shape healthcare. It's all about data extraction. They want as much personal data from as many people as possible."

"Can I meet you back here in five minutes?" Freddie asked, grabbing her purse. "Maybe fifteen."

"Sure." Ben nodded. He was already looking at his phone.

"Is there something you were supposed to tell me?" That's how Freddie began. Did he even know who MemCorps was? Heck, its name was "Freddie!" Then again, she wasn't even sure he'd read her ebook.

"No—I don't think so. Why?"

"There is nothing you'd *like* to tell me." She held her phone close to her ear. She didn't care if anyone was listening. She didn't care if their phones were bugged. She knew he would tell her if he knew. He would, wouldn't he? He was her husband. They were married. He loved her. He loved her more than . . .

"No. I don't think so. Are you okay?"

"I'm fine," Freddie answered. She found herself staring at an empty Google seven-person bike. Someone—no, a group of Googlers—left it sitting in the parking lot beside ChronosCoffee. Freddie thought about the security unit that tracked the Google bikes, those people (okay, men) in white polo shirts who picked them up all over, even in Palo Alto. How did they fit the seven-person bike into the truck? Maybe she could apply for that job; Freddie Flint-Smythe, Google bike tracker. Her husband had never lied to her before. "I'm fine."

Freddie had her notebook open at Chronos when Surya/Rajat walked past. She shut the book quickly. Ben was nowhere to be found. He'd probably walked back to HackerSpace for something. It was definitely a good thing Surya/Rajat hadn't seen them together.

Freddie didn't know if she should show recognition. Should she say something? *How's MemCorps? Where's the office these days? Doing anything illegal or even slightly dodgy at the moment? Still heading to TED, Sellout? Open source anything lately?* They were options. But the agents warned her not to say anything to anyone, not to make contact. Do nothing! She was sick of doing nothing. And now, Freddie had Ben involved.

Ben was a fluke, she told herself. *He'd contacted her. The only one to reach out—wasn't that a sign? Surya—Rajat—might be a sign too, his walking into the coffee shop right at this moment.* But before Freddie could decide, Surya/Rajat waved slightly and walked up to her. She pulled her headphones off.

"Are you *writing*?" He was smirking. "And by hand."

Freddie imagined punching him in the face. That pretty much decided things.

"Yes." *Motherfucker.* "I'm writing. By hand." Did it matter that it was only a list? She put her headphones back on and then tore them off. "You know what, asshole. It's guys like you. You got all *Game of Thrones* on my"—Freddie only minimally whispered the word—"*prototype*. That little video game you made. You were so *proud*. Make the woman pay for her empowerment, her experience, her glasses of wine. Make her pay for wanting to take a cab on her own. You had to go there, didn't you? At first I was disgusted, and then I was just pissed. The thing is, it could have been so great. Only someone like you would think that that was the best use of YOU-KNOW! And now what? Will it help anyone? I'm so sick of misogynists like you. You are such a di—"

But he was gone. Surya/Rajat had turned tail and run out of the coffee shop. A few people stared. One of the baristas, the scruffy guy with the cute man-bun, clapped and winked. Freddie would have enjoyed kissing *him*.

Even if it was the end of the world! Even if she would at some point have to crawl into a cave with both of her children clinging to her back . . . No, maybe not then. Freddie text messaged her husband even after she told herself she might never message him again: *Sometimes I hate this fucking place.*

Reply from Mister: *Hey. Remembered something I was supposed to tell you. I made the vasectomy appointment. Scheduled when you get back from Indiana. You can drive me, right?*

It was all about time. Or, at least, that is what Freddie told Ben when he returned to find her sitting on the curb in front of Chronos.

"You understand how network time protocol is built, right?" Ben asked as he sat down beside her.

"I know enough. But I didn't mean that kind. Maybe it isn't even about time." Freddie was looking at the sky. It was always blue. She was lucky. She was *lucky*! "You're lucky. *Millennial.* What a horrible word. But you know you can do anything. I floundered so much, Ben. I wasted so much time. We just worried about stupid stuff."

"It's never too late to be what you could've been," he said solemnly.

"Don't quote a George Eliot I taught you back to me. Ever. Fuuuck." They sat there, looking at anything that wasn't each other. Freddie said it quietly. "*Might* have. Might have been."

Dinner at home the night before had been a shambles. Everyone talking mean. Fighting.

"You are sucking the life out of me," Freddie said then, her voice breaking. "I do all of this for you. I'm everyone for all of you."

No one paid attention.

Freddie got up from the table. Unload, reload. Minutes went by.

"Come here," Mister said.

She didn't turn around. He wouldn't even let her have another baby. She stood over the sink. She said it quietly and without emotion. "I don't need a hug."

It began. Freddie could feel it. She watched Ben speak. He was rolling. It only took a moment. They were still sitting on the curb in front of Chronos, but everything had changed.

"Our answer is in the time protocol? Really?" Freddie said, finally. "Let me get this—no such thing as time zones. China and California are the same? No matter what time it is, we are all living in the exact same moment. And *that* is where the fault will lie?"

"Yes!" Ben almost cheered. "Exactly. We can change anything we want then and they won't be able to do a thing about it. They'll be live. Public. Welcome to NorCal, assholes. Beware the fucking fault line."

Ben handed stacks of doodles across the table, pages of mapped thought. Lines of code and directions scribbled. His newly showered hair still wet. ". . . and then it came to me," he was saying. Freddie had a vision of what the world could be if the Creatives and the Coders ever banded. "'Freddie' needs zero outages." Multiple sources of multiple selves at multiple times. "We just need to get you to the bastion server."

"Where is that?" Freddie asked.

"In the data center." Ben smiled.

"I'm done," Freddie said. She reached for her bag. "I'm not even sure what I want."

"But I'm going to be there too. Outside. You won't see me, but I'll be there." Ben leaned back. His eyes squinted, then relaxed. She'd never seen him so focused, so sure of himself, so at ease. She couldn't help herself. For a minute, she was proud. "Of course, you could blow up the data center. But you'd have to blow up about five of them. Maybe more."

"I don't want to kill 'Freddie,'" she exhaled towards the ceiling.

Marco Villatoni was right. This could change everything. Try out an idea, a notion, a character, some other self, make a grand shift, make a mistake . . . *wait a minute*. It wouldn't stop people from making mistakes, would it? Humans aren't often the best judges of the benefits of random acts of error. Computers are even worse. *But sometimes it was the mistakes that made me*, Freddie thought.

"You just need to get into the building," Ben said carefully.

"I'm not blowing up a data center." Freddie edited herself: *I'm not blowing up my husband's data center.*

"Wow. It's the real deal." Freddie knew she sounded almost too shocked, too playful as she held the badge bearing her face if not her name. "But how did you . . . ?"

"Don't ask me that," Ben said. "You said you didn't want to use your husband's RFID badge and you'll need one. The Company doesn't screw around with security at their data centers."

Freddie nodded.

"Listen, we need to have a plan."

Serious, Freddie thought. *Okay, Serious Ben. We're not really doing this, but if we were . . .* Ben usually smiled, joked about these kinds of things. He wasn't joking now. Freddie watched him rake his fingers through his curls. She looked at his eyes, at how intent he seemed on this problem. His laptop open, his eyes scanning back and forth from screen to her. She couldn't help it; she kept his gaze on purpose for an extra beat. He nodded, relaxing a bit into a half smile. Freddie thought for an instant about what it would feel like to hold his hand so close on the table.

"You already understand parallel computation?" Ben asked. His voice just above a whisper. She had to look at his lips. "Did you hear me?"

She leaned forward. They both were flushed.

"—neural nets?"

"Like in the brain," she said. His skin was beautiful, like her children's, but different. She wouldn't think of a metaphor. That might be racist. Ben's skin was darker than her husband's, darker than her children's. He was smiling at her now, relaxed. Those eyes.

"Yes," he said. "It is a very loose imitation of neurons in the brain."

"Okay." Freddie noticed he was wearing a clean shirt. This wasn't always the case.

"Honestly," he sighed. "The Company's got this. I mean they're the people who've got Big Data figured out."

Ben waited for a response and, when none came, continued. "Okay,

I want to make sure you understand. Example: 'Freddie' knows you. You tell her everything. She knows your history—what you did and what you do. Knows what you want out of life. She anticipates based on both the past *and* your future goals. Let's say you're buying plane tickets. 'Freddie' could intrinsically understand your seating needs. You want love? Okay. You sit beside your best match on the flight or someone who knows your best match. You want to network? Check. Maybe you want something else—a chance to feel a certain way or have a specific experience, a mile-high situation even."

"It does all that?"

"She does way more than that. And the more people who use 'Freddie,' the smarter she gets," Ben said. "It bothers you. The whole 'she' thing. Sorry."

"Fucking patriarchy." Freddie looked at her hands.

"You've been concerned about the more human aspects of 'Freddie,' right?"

Freddie nodded. *'Freddie" anticipates your every need.*

"It's not just about data or methodology." He was trying to comfort her. "It's about the experience as well. Every click provides . . . well, experience. It is constantly making sense of signals."

"Signs," Freddie said. "It's reading the signs."

Ben looked up at the ceiling. "She certainly is."

Freddie never erases her browser history and her phone is sitting right there. The code you need to open her phone is 4-3-2-1. Go ahead. You can find Freddie's most recent search history for yourself: Alzheimer's treatments nontraditional Breaking Nondisclosure Agreements Are suggested actions by Federal Agents laws Russia Edward Snowden Toto Anonymous Outsourcers Freddie MemCorps

They met at ChronosCoffee on yet another cloudless California day perfumed with honeysuckle. The sun bright, the sky blue, the Redwoods shady. The citrus trees nearly erotic with the weight of their fruit. This is *real* life? Freddie's walk to Chronos seemed to hold all of this out to her, as if saying, "Look at this diverse, ingenious, halcyon valley you are able to call home." *For as long as we can afford the rent*, Freddie thought, walking past two guys smoking in front of the 7/11. Alongside them, she inhaled.

"I've figured it out," Ben said before Freddie even sat down. "Now stay with me. There is a cluster of machines. Multiple operations. No loops. Now, there could be a file, an unmanned delete if time is not the same. At least, I can't imagine . . ." Ben stopped.

He was thinking, and then they looked at one another. "Give me a minute," Ben said. Freddie listened to the conversation at the nearest table. She studied the low braid of the woman at the table beside them. The emo music the baristas had chosen turned up louder. When Ben finally spoke, he spoke just above a whisper. Freddie had to lean close to hear him.

Freddie's head hurt.

"I need a drink," Freddie said. Ben looked towards the line and so did she. All prosperous, interesting, boring, self-absorbed, isolated people waiting in a line to order coffee. "No, I mean a real drink."

Ben thumbed his phone. It wasn't even 10:00 a.m. It was barely 9:30. His face registered shock and then childish thrill. "I'm in."

"I don't even know what's open," she said, as they walked out. There was nothing truly unhealthy here between campuses. They would need wheels. "I don't care if we have to go to BevMo. I want a drink and a cigarette."

"That's funny. I never pegged you as a smoker. I mean, of cigarettes."

"I'm not." *I'm now a healthy motherfucker.* "Look, my car is only a couple blocks away."

They walked the first few blocks in silence.

"What do you want?" Ben asked, suddenly.

"You mean in addition to the do-no-harm, saving-the-world kinds of stuff?" Freddie hated the way she sounded. "Fighting corporate tyranny? Blocking the co-opting of our stories for the purposes of commerce and governmental oversight?"

"No." Ben smiled. "I mean to drink."

"Vodka." She tried to laugh.

They both looked up. The blimp was above them, puttering through the sky, an advertisement for the newest Uniqlo location taut on each enormous side.

"It's funny," Freddie said. "Earlier everything looked beautiful. I'd almost forgotten."

"So vodka." Ben laughed as if this was an appropriate punchline. And then, a little awkwardly, he said, "Good choice. You don't do well with tequila."

She stared at him. They were standing on opposite sides of her car. Doors shut. "I don't get it."

"Tequila. You." Ben chuckled again. "I read it, you know. Your book. Online." He looked a little worried, waiting for her to move. "I mean, of course I read it." He stood there. "You know, that night. You drank all that tequila. It was bad. And then, you know, the other night."

She opened her car door before he could bring up the scene with the bag of pills. "Oh," she said, unlocking his door. "Right."

It was weird enough to have him in the car with her. Someone in the passenger seat. She thought about what music to play and then stopped. *I should have done this alone*, she thought. She put in an old Spin Doctors/Ace of Bass mix.

"I forgot about the 7/11," she said as they drove past. "We could have picked up something there. I'm not thinking well."

"BevMo will have more. More choice. Better choice."

"Is that always the answer?" Freddie moaned. She was angry now. "The tequila. That scene. The other one. Just so you know. I had trouble with loss."

"We all do, Freddie," Ben said. "That's why it's important, right?"

I saw the sign and it opened up my mind.

"Right." About the collective. For the collective. She thought of Marco Villatoni. About the way Ben described the synthesis of Big Data and human intuition. If any version helped someone feel less alone, wasn't it worth it? "I don't know."

"Can I ask you something?" Ben looked nervous.

FUCKNO, Freddie thought. She knew she owed him. And she knew he was uncomfortable. *I don't want to have to take care of you too*, she almost said. *I was your Outsourcer. I'm not anymore. You will never understand.* But Freddie said nothing, staring at the road. What was he even asking?

". . . I've always wanted to know." He was watching her. "I mean, do you still talk to any of them?"

"Who?"

Ben rattled off names.

Freddie smiled. "No, I don't still talk to them." That was easy. She looked in her rearview mirror. They might even be taking pictures now. In this minute.

"Her? Even him?" Ben stuttered. "Or . . . you know. The other guy? Tequila night guy."

"No!" Freddie didn't mean to say it like that, like it was stupid to even ask such a thing. "Of course not." She swallowed hard, her stomach churning. "Listen, I'm not even sure he was real. I mean, really like that." *It was a story. I needed it. Then and later*, she added silently.

El Camino was still full of commuter traffic. People late for work. Impatient. Balancing coffee and phones and the steering wheel. In multiple languages. *The real Braid*, Freddie thought. And that's just in this moment: memory, empathy, anger, time, Ben, the jobs, her children, her husband, her life, El Camino Real.

"It was confusing. Life is confusing. I have no idea what's true and what isn't. Ever. That's why they never should have built all of this on me. I'm the last person to base anything on."

"I don't know," Ben said. "Hey, what ever happened to the mobster guy? I loved that guy. He was great."

"He wasn't a mobster." She wasn't sure this was entirely true. "Or he was the best kind."

"What did that girl call him?"

"Wow." Freddie was shocked. "You really read it?"

"Of course I read it."

They didn't speak for a minute. The sun too bright.

"Nos-tie-esh-ee Moo-sheena. A real man," Freddie said, her throat aching. One of the only Russian phrases she still remembered. She stopped herself before she added: *I'm not even sure my husband read it.* The past is not the present. For a second, she thought Ben might reach over and hold her hand. *Fuck Fuck Fuck.*

"Shit. It's not open," Freddie said, turning off El Camino into the BevMo parking lot. There was nothing to do but wait. She left the keys in the ignition. "He wasn't a mobster. At least, I don't think he was. He was a gentleman," she said quietly. "They all were really."

"But surely you've looked them up, right? I mean, come on! The 'where are they now?' kind of thing. Don't you ever wonder what happened to them?"

"Of course I do. And of course I don't. I have a life, Ben. I have children who need me not just to make them breakfast but to make them well. I don't know how to explain it. I've built something that relies on my being the right person not just some of the time but all of the time. I can't make mistakes now. Not big ones. Not anymore."

"No outages," Ben muttered.

"Stop," Freddie said. "I don't want to think about *it* right now, okay?" Freddie would never say *her*. "But," she sighed, "to answer your question. Sure, I think of them. Sometimes."

Okay.

"Let's walk over there," Freddie said, pointing to the Korean market, "and come back. It'll be open by then." She wanted out of the car.

It was weird to walk around the store with Ben. It felt too much like a first date. They grabbed fresh juices and rice crackers. Ben laughed loudly. He bought mints. Freddie sweated. *We're like colleagues*, she thought. *This is what happens when you work with people. That's all this is.*

"In a couple years we'll probably be able to buy weed here," Ben said over the magazines at the checkout. Freddie tried to smile along with him. Nothing about this moment felt good or right. She was nauseous and lightheaded. *You're not doing anything wrong. You're buying snacks.*

"Do you want some? We just need to swing by HackerSpace. Or my place." Ben slowed down. "I mean . . . I can hook you up."

Oh God. What am I doing? Freddie thought. *I'm too old for this. Ben and his puppy face. Ben and his brain.* "No. Vodka works fine. Perfect with this." She held up her green juice, hands shaking, and pushed the door.

Later, Freddie would return to this moment. She would wonder how it could happen. She replayed it, edited it, changed all of the options available, and more often than not, rewound back to the moment Ben had proven his interest. He hadn't just read her memories, her ebook; he knew them. And this had, in some way, proven to Freddie that he knew her. Did her husband even know that she'd almost killed herself? That she had, not once but a few times in that year she'd written about, gotten to that specific place where her life seemed beyond discovery. *How do we misplace our own lives?* Freddie wondered as she drove that day. But even more, she wondered how her husband might not know she asked this question and Ben did.

They pulled into the parking lot on the border of the Superfund site next to Middlefield. She could leave her car here if she needed. *Come back later to get it*, Freddie thought. She could walk home. Walk to get the kids. And Ben could walk back to Chronos or HackerSpace or wherever and continue his day, his life.

I'm one of the people parking mid-day, Freddie thought. *Afternoon Delighters*, her husband called them. People they'd disturbed by walking past, with kids on scooters, laughing, bickering, talking loudly. A joke between parents—*oh happy family*—about the cars and the people sitting in them; furtive looks and smirks from the parents, ignorance and disinterest from the kids. Drug deals or affairs under the golden California light. You can do a lot at a constant seventy degrees.

"Smug," Freddie said, accidentally aloud.

She couldn't remember the last time she'd had a drink before 4:00. Not even a Bloody Mary these days, not with the weekends they'd had this year. She wouldn't be able to function, let alone run. The headache would make the onslaught harder.

"I wish girls now were like you. Like you are and like you were then," Ben said, his fingers drumming on his knees. "I mean, you're like me. You had all the same fears and stuff. You wanted to do the right thing. I just wish girls were like you."

"Girls now are better." Freddie was staring at the dirt through the window. "They're more confident. Smarter. I was so scared."

I still am, she thought.

"I can't do this," Freddie said. Willa knew, didn't she? Right from the start. *Why didn't I make more mistakes then?* This wasn't the Freddie she thought she was going to be even a few minutes earlier. She thought she could be someone else, even just someone who drank vodka mixed with cold-pressed green juice before 11:00 a.m. "I've always been afraid of something."

The vodka bottle was just sitting there, unopened, between them. She sighed and opened her juice. Ben nodded and opened his.

"I don't know. You can seem pretty badass to me . . . at times."

"That's just the way I wrote it." They both took drinks of juice. "And for what?" Freddie continued, wiping her mouth. *Bullshit*, she thought. *I did it for the money. I did it for a home. I did it to pay off my son's medical bills. I did it because I wanted to make something that was mine. I did it because I was good at it.*

"Making better choices. Learning from everyone's mistakes," Ben said and then self-corrected. "*Possible* mistakes."

"Is that a good thing?"

"Sure."

"Why?" She looked at him. She made herself. They both hated eye contact today. "Why are you helping me?" *I only want to hear the answer if it doesn't make me feel worse*, she thought. "I wrote you a book. This affects you too. That's why, right?" He was looking right at her. "Ben, you have a lot to lose and nothing to gain. Trust me."

"This isn't just for you." Ben looked down. "I mean, of course, I would do this for you. But this is bigger too. This is what I do." Face flushed. "Information. Power. This isn't just about you." His eyes found hers. "Even if it is."

He lifted up his sleeve. There, tattooed around his upper bicep were the words: *An enemy is a friend is a lover is a mother is a terrorist is an enemy is a friend.*

Her words, words from *her* memoir!

"My favorite quote." Those eyes.

"You got it tattooed?" *Then, I could be a mess*, Freddie thought. *I could lie and cheat and be dumb and it didn't really mean anything. The drama could always be beneficial in the end.* Joan's voice: "This is just something else you can write about." What doesn't kill you gives you fodder. *Then, I would have fallen in love with you just for the tattoo.*

"We've all done things we regret," he began.

"No. Not yet. Not really."

"Sometimes it's worth it," he said.

She stared out the front window at the ground and the sky. The only ground left undeveloped in the entire neighborhood. The place her children thought of as *The Soil*.

"Fuck," Freddie sighed and then laughed, blushing. They sat there, the word between them, looking out at the unplowed land. Damaged. Fallow. "It must be worth a fortune. Even if it is toxic."

"Someone big bought that empty semiconductor place and this land.

It's a new secret housing project. Corporate housing for the luckiest of the tech workers." Ben frowned. "*Project* . . . well, anyway. Funny, because someday soon everything is going to get outsourced. This place will be a ghost town in five years."

Freddie felt numb.

"You look so sad."

She realized too late that she needed to explain. "It's where we walk. It's where they practice riding bikes." *Home*.

"You were my voice, Freddie. Please, let me finish. You know me better than anyone. We're kind of part of each other." Ben had turned in his seat.

He is going to kiss me, Freddie thought.

Freddie heard someone talking loudly. She turned her head just in time. The guy from the neighborhood walking Pebbles with his phone. Their respective leashes. What *was* his name?

"Shit," she said, leaning into her seat. Her car smelled of sweat and day-old seashells and food. A Volvo station wagon (*you can always live in a station wagon*)—a family car! Of course he knew her car. Pebbles probably even knew her car. The only car in the neighborhood with bumper stickers. She was already practicing it in her head. *Thank you for being my friend. Thank you for being the person I needed.*

Ben was leaning towards her, but the seatbelt caught him. She said it just in time.

She didn't have the courage to look at his face. Her hand accidentally gripped the bottle instead of the shift.

She'd save the vodka for later.

Freddie found it while unloading her groceries. It was in the second zippered bag between the boxes of sushi and the bottles of Pranqster. Delivered. It looked like a map. X marked the spot. *You will be here* in the middle of a data center. On the back there was an embossed invitation with a date and time and words typed almost like the fortune in a cookie: SFO parking lot. Space 23B. Passenger seat. Say your name. Follow the map. Take the badge!

And then in red ink: Good luck.

"I'm working on a writing project." Freddie rehearsed this line. She was leaving for Indiana at the end of the week. "I need to write my character into a data center."

Mister nodded, taking a sip. He had gotten used to these kinds of questions in marriage to Freddie Flint-Smythe.

"They have a cleaning crew, right? They need someone to vacuum." Freddie smiled. She didn't want to be false. She wasn't going to lie—*not really*. Not a *real* lie. She wanted him to say something so she could say something and they could do this together and it could be them against the world just like it had always been. "That could be a way in, right?"

"But they wouldn't let a cleaning crew onto the DC floor."

"It's not in DC. It's in . . . some kind of desert region."

"No," he laughed. "DC. Data Center."

He took another sip of his coffee. He never read her work and that was okay. Freddie didn't want to be married to herself. "Your character could be a vendor. But if it were a woman, she'd have to dress kind of slutty. All the vendor ladies dress slutty."

"And the guys?" For whatever reason, it didn't bother Freddie that her husband had noticed this fact. Actually, it made her proud. She had trained him to give her these kinds of details.

"Oh, the guys just wear polos."

"But this would be at the DC," Freddie continued. "Not a sales call. Would a woman—this character—would she still dress slutty?"

"No, probably not. You're right. She'd probably wear a vendor polo shirt too. And khakis. Never jeans. And they always iron them."

So that's my plan, Freddie thought. At least she wouldn't have to do it in a push-up bra and heels. For a minute she thought of *La Femme Nikita* and pictured herself in a doorway. That might have been fun. She thought about Jennifer Garner (now there was a celebrity Freddie knew she could be friends with). Freddie could almost see the list begin: *Get a polo shirt.*

She looked at her husband, drinking his coffee, scrolling through the news on his phone. She drank her smoothie and called up to the kids, "Breakfast!" Then Freddie played out a different scene in which no one was dressed in old jogging shorts and a stained, free Hadoop tee shirt. Instead, Freddie would be costumed in a snazzy two-piece pajama set. Blue and white stripes. Monogram in navy.

Begin Scene. "Why didn't you tell me?" "I couldn't." "What do you mean 'you couldn't'? I could get fired. We could lose everything. It is my job to provide for this family." Drinks flying, hot and cold, stopping in mid-air. *End Scene*.

How had Freddie forgotten that she kept secrets too?

She'd been searching online all day between duties. Nothing. Nerd humor tee shirts on Café Press weren't going to cut it. Freddie knew what she needed, and for some reason, data center vendors weren't selling their company-logoed shirts online. Freddie stared at the logo. It was easy to find. Okay, fairly easy. She'd found the data center online, imaged it, and began the process of negotiating the building. Mapping the doors and rooms. The entry desk.

Not only did she find a list of The Company's DC vendors online, she also found their logoed swag inside the center's front office using Maps. On a water bottle left on a table. On an exercise ball rolled next to a chair. *I'll just have to make the polo shirt myself*, Freddie decided, all while thinking: *I'm not really going to do this. But if I was, this is exactly how I would do it*.

Freddie could feel the magic again. That mojo; that source stuff; that luck. But it felt wrong too. *I'm doing something I'm not supposed to and it feels really, really great*. A feeling Freddie remembered equally well.

So just before the first pick-up that same day, Freddie primed three white polo shirts online and stopped at JoAnn's. Freddie went through the list of items she needed: stabilizer, floss x3, sealant. She would put her fingers on the stitched portions and tear away the stabilizer carefully. *Careful* not to disturb the stitching. *Maybe* using a fusible mesh stabilizer over the whole backing? But then she'd have to be really careful. *Stiffness*. If the logo looked too stiff, she'd be in real trouble.

Freddie wanted to start immediately, but she would have to wait until the next time everyone was out of the house. She couldn't risk someone walking in on her. She didn't want to lie.

She also needed to stop asking Ben for help. Anyway, he hadn't called either. "You can still be dangerous," Freddie reassured herself.

Later, almost evening, after Freddie had hidden all of her purchases under their bed, as Mister arrived home: "Oh, I almost forgot," he said.

"We got something at work today. Just from one of the vendors."

"What vendor?" Freddie made herself ask. She didn't turn around. She was at the oven, hands hot-padded, lifting a lasagna. She stopped. She didn't move. This was it. This was exactly how the magic worked, tumbling, capturing her and taking her with it. She could feel it about to begin. About to consume her.

"Just a storage one. If you don't want it you can take it to Goodwill or I can use it as a rag in the garage."

And Freddie's heart hurt. It actually hurt. Why had she not thought of the Goodwills of Silicon Valley? Ha. They were lousy—just plastic kid toys and tech swag. She shut the oven. He held the balled-up fabric to her. She could see it out of the corner of her eye. It was white. She couldn't breathe. It wasn't going to be a polo shirt. It was going to be a tee shirt or a logoed stocking cap or acrylic gloves with pads at the fingers so you could scroll during winter break. It was going to be something she couldn't use. She could barely look at it for fear it might actually be the shirt she wanted.

She set the lasagna down and willed herself to look up. *Stuff like this only happens in movies*, she thought.

"Not great for working out in," Mister said. "It's funny. We got two sizes, an extra large and a medium. Tony was naughty and said to Frank, 'Hey, that still works out well for you.'"

"I don't get it," Freddie said. She was trying not to stare. She felt like she might throw up. *It's all working out now*, Freddie thought. *I'm lucky. I'm a bad person, but I'm lucky*, she thought as she stared at the polo shirt in front of her. She also noticed that she'd purchased the wrong shade of red. Bad embroidery floss choice. Yes, Freddie was lucky.

"His partner is kind of big."

"That's mean," she made herself say. She made herself smile.

"It is," he said, smiling. Walking towards her, kissing her. He never kissed her when he came home. "You smell good. You smell like my wife."

"Like lasagna and cookies," she mumbled. He kissed her harder.

"Maybe."

"You smell like air conditioning," she said, feeling guilty. *I'm a bad person. A very bad person.* She was getting exactly what she thought she wanted.

88

"My husband is supposed to smell like sweat and bicycle grease."

"Where are the kids?"

"Hansa and Miss"—she wouldn't say *The Nanny* like he always did; she wouldn't—"Manvinder invited them over. They're decorating cookies. I was just over there, but the timer went off." She lifted her phone. "And I had to come pull out the dinner."

"It could take a few minutes," he said, kissing her neck.

"It could."

They had sex in bed all the time now. And that was fine. The floor was hard! And that counter was never as fun as it looked in the movies.

They were up the stairs and naked before a minute had passed.

"I need to brush my teeth," she said.

"No you don't," he mumbled between kisses. "Then I'd have to." She was on her back. He was on top of her. It was embarrassingly clichéd how much she enjoyed it that way.

"I've missed you," he said.

"What do you mean?"

"I don't know."

"I'm here," she said.

All she ever had to do was look at his arms and hipbones. To put her hands down his shoulders and onto his back. And he was everything again.

eight

The email appeared in her Inbox as Freddie waited to board her first plane. She'd been sitting in SFO since dawn, intermittently feeling guilty and thinking about the data center. She knew a SatCar might actually be waiting for her in the parking lot even now, but the date and time were specific.

Freddie hadn't called or messaged Ben, and she noted, he hadn't called or messaged her. She assumed the invitation came from him, but she didn't want to think about it. *I have enough to go on.* Now, it was just about timing and choices. She looked out the airport's long wall of glass. The sun was rising over the mountains. She checked her watch. They weren't even awake yet.

She watched the people reading *Consumer Reports* and *Women's Health*. She listened to conversations. People wearing their team colors, people going home, people not from Cali. *Why can't I have another baby?*

She wouldn't call Mister. She wouldn't text him.

She looked at her phone, and a message appeared, prompting her to check an old email account. Freddie tried logging into fabfredD@yahoo.com, a remnant carrier of her past, but she couldn't remember the password. Fourth time's a charm:

From: nadiebee <nadiebee@aol.com>
To: Freddie <fabfredD@yahoo.com>
Subject: Re: Hi

Hi Freddie -

I'm in the process of moving & I still have that old wooden desk. Was just wondering if you wanted it? I think I asked you the last time I moved but you may have had a change of heart so thought I'd ask again.

Hope you're doing well,
Nadine

Nadine was still using AOL? Okay. Freddie smiled. Who only moves twice in all these years? It made Freddie feel old in only the good ways. It was easy to be gracious. Freddie replied. She sighed. Everything was flowing and she didn't want to ask why.

"Freddie, what a surprise!" She looked up to find Marco Villatoni standing in front of her. "You're going with us to the conference after all!" Marco was grinning, standing there in the middle of SFO, people everywhere.

"Oh, Mr. . . . Marco," Freddie stuttered. *What was he doing here? Now?*
"I wish I could. I'm visiting my grandmother in the Midwest."

The plane tickets. Today. Departure. Of course.

"That's right." He nodded, his face sincere. "She had a surgery, didn't she?"

"That was my son." Freddie bit her lip. "It's confusing. It's been a confusing time. In fact, I can't believe you're actually here in front of me." It was like a dream, or a movie, or a dream in a movie. People in places you don't expect them to be. People *exactly* where they're supposed to be.

"I have to go catch my plane," he said and smiled. "Good to see you, Freddie. Best of luck."

"Why did you sell?" She didn't care who heard.

Marco Villatoni was walking away. He could have pretended, but he didn't. He turned around and walked back to Freddie.

"History." He shrugged. "I want us all to have a voice. I want everyone to be heard."

"But—"

"Freddie, the stories we tell are created through a social process. There are moments that are crucial in this creation. I'm not just talking about that moment when something happened, I'm also talking about that moment when it was processed, that moment when it was given shape and form—a later time, perhaps much later. But I'm also talking about another moment and another and another." He looked so happy. "Freddie, I'm talking about when it is shared. When it is remembered. When it is told and retold or reread. Now multiply that. We need to tell our stories. We need to be heard. And for that to happen, we need the biggest microphone." He stopped, his eyes tired, still smiling. "Lecture finished. I've a plane to catch." Then he leaned closer to Freddie. "Truthfully, this was the right time for me to tell *this* story. Maybe not perfectly or in the way I thought it, but—" He began to walk away but turned his head to call back to her. "Good luck, my dear! Safe journey."

From: nadiebee <nadiebee@aol.com>
To: Freddie F-S <freddief_s@gmail.com>
Subject: Re: Hi

I would love to catch up if you have time.

I'm halfway, Freddie thought, running to board her connection in Minneapolis. And there they were, the Midwesterners, waiting patiently. Smiling. *Oh, ye good people with crockpots*, Freddie thought. *I'm one of you, aren't I? Oh ye land of the past, ye pale doughy people who smile. Smile at me again.*

Freddie was listening to a meditation podcast.

Respond to what arrives. Learn, once again, to be open. So, as Freddie waited in line to board her second and final flight of the day, leading and following her kith and kin, she answered.

But there was no response when Freddie switched her phone out of Airplane Mode upon landing in Indianapolis. *Oh well. It was the gracious thing to do*, Freddie told herself. She looked out the window at the flat black Indiana night.

Freddie kept walking, but slower. She knew no one would be there waiting on the other side. No Dad holding a paperback, dressed in khaki shorts, wearing a sweater in the air conditioning and his silver glasses. No Mom in capris and a cardigan with her big black statement frames and her watery eyes. Freddie was grown now. She didn't need to be met. "I love them," Freddie said. She was tired. She said it out loud in front of her rental car. Back home again in Indiana. It's what the signs all said. *Welcome Home.* You are here.

I've written this before, Freddie thought. *Maps and yurts. Homes for nomads.* They'd been taught to call them *yurta* in Peace Corps, the Russian word, but it was Turkic in origin and referred not to the building itself but to the imprint that shell of a moveable house—the accordion-like framework— left in the dirt after it was moved. Because that was the most important part: these were homes for transients. *What about a yurt?* Freddie wished she could talk Mister and the children into one. But where would they build it? Cupertino?

Something named only after it was gone. But even that line was somewhere, backed up. And not just in one data center, but in several. In Kansas and North Carolina and Sweden and Iceland and Brazil and Bangladesh. Make a map, if you like. Because we all want to leave some trace in the dust.

Freddie was in the back bedroom at Gram's when she heard it.

"Freddie isn't taking anything?" her sister-in-law asked.

"They'd just end up giving it away," Joan answered. "They move too often."

Of course we do. Should she show them her photo stream? The pictures between her children:

Welcome to Middlefield, my family. Where people are living in RVs parked along the side of the road, one after another—if only Freddie could get Mister to consider one, but their two-bedroom depressed him enough. This was the truth. Rentals were only for the rich. And the rich were just middle class tech.

Later, Freddie replayed the scenes. Visiting Gram in the nursing home. Watching her brothers carry furniture while she cried. And the way it was later when they all were eating, the children vying for her attention. At that moment, she was no one's mother. *I'm just their aunt*, Freddie thought. *This is how my life would have been.*
This is not my life.

Saturday. Her brothers and their families were now gone. The end in sight. Freddie was homesick. *Ca-al-i-fornia. Let me see the folks I dig. Might even kiss a sunset pig. California, coming home.*
I should want to go to a movie, definitely the bookstore, Freddie thought. *I should want to visit my old friends and see their babies.* But she didn't. She wanted to spend time with her parents and Gram or drive by herself or call Mister and tell him she loved him. How it sometimes surprised her that she could love him more the better she knew his faults, the better her own faults were revealed. But why didn't she think of this beside him?

She walked around the neighborhood and it wasn't even real. *My alternate lives*, Freddie thought. *All of them. I am not who you think I am. I am no longer the person I was.* It was grass she'd described, the plotted-out yards, as if she were walking between her own words. Nothing was really linear. Sets kept changing. Like in a dream. *I'm here, but I'm also someplace else.* That's how she felt when she was writing the memoirs. She was Freddie and she was someone else.

Freddie looked at the clouds. *These clouds I know*, she thought. *I want to be led. Send me a sign.* She took a picture of the sky. *Dear Children, these are real clouds.* Her picture sent into her camera roll, into storage, and a few minutes later, to another cloud, an invisible/not invisible Company Cloud. It would be on their screen now in the living room back in Middlefield. Her children could look at *these* clouds because their father was so smart. *Her Company man*; Freddie was proud of his work. Freddie opened her email and saw it:

> From: nadiebee <nadiebee@aol.com>
> To: Freddie F-S <freddief_s@gmail.com>
> Subject: Re: Hi
>
>
> Sorry Freddie - unfortunately I have not entered the 21st century & do not have either a CoPhone or email access at my apartment!!! Came in to catch up on work and found this!
>
> If tonight works for you I could do that. Maybe meet around 5:30? There's a Starbucks on 96th street.
> I know it's not a hip coffee joint but it's fairly easy access for both of us. Let me know & sorry about missing you yesterday!
>
> From: Freddie F-S <freddief_s@gmail.com>
> To: nadiebee <nadiebee@aol.com>
> Subject: Re: Hi
> Are you kidding me, Starbucks is perfect! See you soon.
>
> Sent from my CoPhone

About fifteen minutes after she finally arrived, Nadine said, "You're still so the same. It's funny." She laughed. "No, it's good."

This pleased Freddie. Just as it pleased her that she knew Nadie would be at least fifteen minutes late. Just as it pleased her that she hadn't told anyone that she was headed to this Starbucks at this time to witness a memory. Just as it pleased her that Nadie had aged more than she had.

But then Freddie began: *Don't I seem better than I was? Aren't I in the middle of my toned-even-after-children prime? The Prime of Ms. Freddie Flint-Smythe?*

What role was Freddie playing now? In her thrift store shift dress, her legs sticking to the chair's lap, the Indiana sun on her bare arms, her hair piled on her head, sunglasses covering half her face. *The Ex-Girlfriend.* Freddie sipped her iced (unsweetened) green tea and smiled—everything could be simple. Keep it simple. Don't add more layers. But whom was she playing? Was this *her* decades earlier? Freddie doubted it. She was never this cool.

"It's funny," Nadie said. "You got everything you ever wanted. It seems like kind of a fairy tale really." And then, in a different way: "You always wanted children."

"Tell me about you," Freddie asked, not wanting to dwell on the *fairy tale*. "How's Kelly?" It was nice to ask. Of course, Freddie had no idea what Kelly actually looked like or who she really was. They'd never met. Freddie heard rumors, of course, descriptions back then from mutual friends. This happens when you've been dumped.

"She's good," Nadine said. "She and her partner have a baby."

"I'm confused."

"We broke up about . . . let me see . . . three years ago?" Nadine leaned back in her chair. "We just became like roommates. Like best friends. We're still friends."

"I'm so sick of hearing about lesbian bed death," Freddie said. "It happens in all relationships. You have to try. Everyone has lulls. You just have to keep it alive." Freddie didn't want to dial herself back. Didn't want to cover up again. "Women are just lazy sometimes. They want the fantasy."

Nadine was laughing. "You're right."

"It's not fun losing my street cred, Nadie. I don't mean to sound anti-feminist. I hate that. You know how much I hate that." Freddie was laughing.

"Could've been my fault." Nadine looked a little sad.

"Don't be silly." Freddie smiled. "I'm sorry about Kelly, though."

"My mom was so mad at me when we broke up. Kelly and me. She sounded just like you did just now. I told her maybe I needed to sow my oats. She said I was acting like Dad."

"No wonder your mom was mad." *Your mother never liked me*, Freddie thought. *Me?!* "How many times *do* you need to sow your oats, Nadine?"

"Well . . ." Nadine smiled. "I'm ready to settle down now." And Nadine told the story. Great partner with a teenage son. They were buying a house together. Starting a life. Becoming a family. "Can you see me as a stepmother?"

"Yes, I can. You're going to be great. I'm really happy for you." Freddie meant it.

"Heck, I almost forgot." Nadie got up and walked over to her car. Freddie noticed it was no longer a vehicle she recognized. Nadie pulled out a tube from the backseat. "Look what I found."

Freddie opened it and unrolled.

"You're kidding me," she laughed. "You kept this?" It was her old Virginia Woolf poster.

"You used to hang it up first thing when we'd move."

"I remember."

Freddie thought of Gram. *What am I leaving behind?* Stacks of old journals? A worn copy of *Where There Is No Doctor*? Trash. Recycling. It wasn't even her life. It wasn't even what she was most proud of. It wasn't even what mattered. Maybe Gram had it figured out. Everything short term, no memories impacting moments. *But this was the feeling you'd miss.*

"So, how's *your* mom?"

Freddie laughed. She laughed so hard tears began to grow. "She's good. Dad just retired from the ministry. I don't know what their plans are next."

Nadine's face became serious, exactly the way Freddie remembered. Those dual frown lines between her eyes. *They used to trouble me*, Freddie thought. It almost made Freddie smile. *I feel like a grandmother, so fond, so pleased.*

"You know," Nadine started. Freddie tried not to look too pleasant. "I have to tell you. I've always wanted to tell you. I feel, *felt*, a lot of guilt over the years about the way you came home."

Freddie couldn't help it. She smiled. "Nadie, it was the greatest gift in the world." *I needed someone to break my heart.* "No, really. It was the way things were supposed to happen."

"You were homeless!" Nadine still looked worried. She held on tight to her frappuccino. "You had nowhere."

"Nadie, really. It helped me grow up. I needed it."

"Still." The frown lines were gone. Nadine wasn't worried anymore. She'd said what she wanted to say.

Right there, Freddie thought. *End Scene*. Remnant shards of guilt, happiness, joy, change. It was all there. Everyone deserved as much.

"It's funny." Nadine shook her head. "It's like the Universe kept reminding me of you lately. Like I was being led. Books you always talked about, songs, Everything but the Girl, stuff like that kept repeating. I think that's why I emailed."

"Maybe you were led," Freddie said, her voice low. "Maybe we both were."

I want to follow the map. I want to leave something in the dust. I want to be led. Freddie had always wanted an epiphany. The ultimate sign. It was almost neon bright above her head: *I am here.*

nine

What actually happened and what Freddie expected to happen were often two wildly disparate scenes. A driver in a flat cap holding a sign? Is that what Freddie expected when she arrived back at SFO?

Instead, Freddie pulled out her phone and switched it out of Airplane Mode. Not only did she have a text message that included a map to her car, she now had an app automatically appear on her phone that let her follow the progression of her trip on screen, from airport gate to car to data center in the middle of nowhere.

Freddie had exactly five hours until they expected her home. She could almost walk from SFO to Middlefield in that time. She hadn't lied, exactly. *I will never lie to you.* Freddie told herself that she didn't know for certain if she was actually going towards the car until she, onscreen, saw that she was.

The SatCar was waiting exactly where the map said it would be. As Freddie stood beside the white Prius, she wondered where the screen was to enter her password. She searched the exterior of the car. She put her fingers, her palms, all over it. And it was only while Freddie was lying on the pavement looking under the car that she heard her phone beep again from the depths of her tote bag. Beneath the hidden polo shirt and khakis, under the handheld travel steamer, hand cleaner, and what remained of the gluten-free snacks—her phone sat, tossed back in after seeing the car in front of her on the map. The screen lit up. *Make no mistake*, Freddie thought. *I'm really doing this.* She entered her password and thus: the SatCar. The two USB drives were waiting for her on the passenger seat. One green and one red.

The data center was just over an hour from San Francisco, in a town called Franklinville. Basically, Franklinville *was* data centers. They're all there. Facebook, Apple, The Company, Amazon, and Microsoft take up most of the land in Franklinville in the form of vast buildings with nothing surrounding them but parking lots. There's an Applebee's a mile down the road; a Day's Inn about three miles further. And that's it.

"Freddie" was stored alongside all the other data. Purchases made, people contacted, search terms backed up. Server racks in rows. Air conditioning. A buzzing heard for miles.

The SatCar drove towards Franklinville, and Freddie sat in the passenger seat, watching the road and the lines the orchards made *as well as* the animated road on her screen. She looked out at the mountains and the valleys and the glassy reservoirs and then at their green and brown and blue equivalents. She updated her satellite location often so she could watch herself at exactly where she was—*I shouldn't have to keep updating.*

She tried to send Ben a thank you text—a *Thx*—for the car and the map and the badge and the plan. For the USB drives. For everything. He'd been a good friend. She pressed *Send* but the upload was incomplete. Blocked by mountains, Freddie assumed.

She passed a reservoir on the right, just before the first big range leading out of exurbia. Freddie imagined a scene where the massive earthquake or bomb or terrorist plot would break the enormous dam wall and water would come pouring out and the SatCar would have to go fast, faster than fast, and they would barely make it to the top. The road and cars populated by extras and any ugly actors washed away. Gone. While Freddie, finally at the top, stepped out of the car like some latter-day Noah, holding a printed copy of Everything, Mister and their children holding on to her, their faces grimy but grateful.

But Freddie was alone in the SatCar.

Thirty minutes in and the car pulled off the freeway and parked at a rare gourmet gas station. It offered up a Starbucks, fairly clean restrooms, and a pleasant variety of snacks (*Larabars? Out here? You have to love California*). After using the restroom and looking through the snacks, Freddie tried to order her drink.

"I'm sorry, ma'am," the youth said in his unpressed khakis. "We're all out of tea."

It was too hot for a coffee, even an iced one. But Freddie was exhausted. Indiana was three hours ahead of California, and she'd had to wake up in the middle of the night to get her here. *You are here.* "I'll just take this then." She held up an overpriced bottle of water.

It was when Freddie got back into the car that she found them. What should have been the glove box had popped open. Two chilled bottles were waiting for her. The labels read: *Remembrance Green Tea*. No ingredients list, just one word: *unsweetened*.

Did it open when the car went off? Freddie wondered. Or perhaps when she'd stepped out of the car? Maybe it was the shift in movement? *Don't think. Just drink.* Exactly what she did. And why did she? Was it because Freddie was worn out from little sleep and large anxiety? Did she just expect snacks to appear after a morning in airplanes? Or was it the fact that she didn't want to think too deeply when what she desired inexplicably faced her? The truth? Freddie was tired of questions.

It tasted good. Exactly the kind of green tea Freddie liked: earthy, very green, slightly bitter, with a hint of citrus. Of course, she would have preferred it over ice. The taste was intense. She drank the first bottle and started on the second. She must have been thirsty. The bottles were cold and fit well in her hand. Freddie found herself watching the bottle, watching the liquid in the bottle, and only later realizing that she was in the SatCar's passenger seat with her seatbelt on, the doors closed, back on the road.

Everything tasted and smelled greener, and Freddie found herself listening to song after song of great music, her dream soundtrack, and it was all there around her in the SatCar. Freddie pressed the windows down.

"But I used to dance!" Freddie screamed into the wind and the fields with too many penned-in cows. Not mom dance with purses after too many drinks on a Thursday night after tuck-in. No. *I used to dance.* Hot, sweaty. In pleather pants and a bikini top, with candyflip hair. *I used to dance!*

Freddie pictured her children. Their lives. Time. *I just want more*, Freddie thought. *Time*. But there was something else and Freddie couldn't quite remember what that was, like a dream unable to be recalled.

The screen inside the SatCar flicked on, and Freddie's eyes fluttered. At first she thought it was Rosemary dressed as *Middlemarch*'s Dorothea Brooke, spouting that line, "The growing good of the world is partly dependent on unhistoric acts." And then, smaller, ever smaller, like a doll, posed, Rosemary now dressed normally, saying, "If you're given a story, Freddie, it's your duty to write it. It's your duty to write it for the people who cannot."

Freddie stared. Rosemary was wearing her own clothing, beautifully accessorized, standing on a stage. "Empathy." Rosemary paused. "It begins in the home. But it doesn't need to stay there. The home is ground zero for revolution."

But this wasn't Rosemary. It just looked a little like her, but it was someone else. Someone telling a story. Freddie knew she wasn't really alone. She understood that if she needed help, she just had to say the word.

Before Freddie could focus, the screen clicked off. The music faded away. Freddie realized the windows were back up, with the air conditioning on full blast. She felt cold.

"Freddie?" she asked finally. The space between them disappeared. There was an answer. A woman's voice.

"I am here."

The screen beeped, and "Freddie" woke up. A different automated voice said, "Fifteen minutes until your destination. We hope you enjoyed your salvia tea. One of our prototypes. Your destination will be on the right."

Salvia? Shit. What is happening to me?

Look at Freddie's phone. Look at her search terms: alzheimer's treatments non-traditional salvia Alzheimer's overnight oats alameda real estate. Freddie had been doing research the night before. She'd used up her data plan as her parents slept, as she waited to leave to drive to the airport.

"Freddie?" It was easier somehow this time.

"I am here."

"I've been driving on fucking salvia?"

"You have been a passenger."

Freddie searched the interior of the car certain she'd find a camera.

"If I end up on YouTube—" She'd be just another person doing something completely boring and then falling over, twitching, and waking up as if everything was all hunky-dory. "This is *not* hunky-dory. Holy shit. And I am not fucking Annie Hall."

"No, you're not." The voice seemed to hold a smile.

Freddie took a deep breath. "We've got a data center to break into." Silence. "Freddie?"

"I am here."

It was at the first security outpost where Freddie almost lost her nerve. The initial barrier was automated. *If the bollards go down. If I get through. Then I'm actually meant to do this.* The badge worked.

At the second outpost, it worked again and the guard motioned for Freddie to continue. The SatCar pulled into a spot in the farthest corner of an empty parking lot. There were only four other cars for miles, and they were all next to the building's entrance. Not exactly inconspicuous.

Freddie changed into her khakis (now slightly wrinkled) and polo shirt, again looking for a camera, some green light gleaming. She tossed her sunglasses into her bag, her eyes burning as she stepped into the heat and bright sunshine. *They'll make you check your bag so leave it in the car*, "Freddie" had advised her. *And they'll trust you more if they see your eyes.* For once, she carried so little. Earphones and USB drives in her pocket, map folded in hand. Badge on. Freddie walked at least a mile over parking lots towards the front door. She treaded on six painted Evacuation Assembly Area circles as she closed first one eye and then the other to the sun. And then, just for a minute, Freddie closed both eyes.

Freddie opened her eyes. She could see her server. The only one for miles with a keyboard.

She began to count backwards. *Ten. Nine. Eight.* It was almost time. She knew what would happen if she stepped out too early. If they caught her. *Four. Three. Two. This is Freddie*, she thought. *But I'm someone else.* Before she even stepped out, she knew.

"Freddie?" she whispered.

"I am here," came the voice through her earbuds.

"But I don't want to be here."

"Where do you want to be?"

They both knew the answer. Freddie remembered the agents telling her to *do nothing*. She didn't know how. She was sick of people telling her not to follow her instincts even if they led her here, right into the middle of the most depressing place she'd ever been. Freddie looked around her. The data center was freezing cold, pure sound. It felt heartless, soulless. She wanted to keep imagining all those stories in the sky instead of here.

"How do you feel?" *Tell me your story.*

Freddie was silent.

"This is what you do when you get replaced," said the voice. "You make a mixed tape. You pick up donuts and chocolate milk and arrive unexpectedly at their house at 6 a.m., exhausted and a little bit high." The voice paused. "And, sometimes, you beg."

"I wrote that," Freddie gasped. "About being dumped. Not about this."

"The options were updated. Chocolate milk would make you sick now."

That woman on the stage, Freddie thought suddenly. "The woman talking before, on stage. That was me?"

Freddie knew this was true before the answer came. That woman—she was older, but Freddie recognized her own face, her own voice. What had the older woman said? Something about the home. *Freddie.*

Her earbuds clicked. "I am here."

The voice was distorted. And it wasn't even important anymore; Freddie just wanted out of this building. The answers weren't here. She wanted to get home as fast as she could.

"Remember why you wrote it in the first place."

"I wanted to give them a house," Freddie whispered into the noise. She started laughing. The tea probably wasn't helping matters. "It's ridiculous, but that's why." It was almost a lie, an easier kind of truth, and she was sick of those. "I wanted to give them something that might last longer—"

"You're running the wrong way."

"I don't care."

"You once told me that you always wanted to live in an action movie."

Freddie couldn't listen anymore. She pulled out her earbuds and started running. She could hear steps behind her even with the noise inside the data center. They were coming fast. She turned the corner, and instead of another row of aisles, she saw a small room. She rushed in and the door shut behind her.

It looked to be some sort of break room. Empty water bottles and three Chipotle napkins on the table. Freddie ran to the far wall, far from the windows, and slid underneath a table, her chest on fire, her head pounding.

Freddie knew that sound. The door opened and the light switched on. She willed her eyes open. Two pairs of legs in jeans were walking towards her. A pair of classic Pumas and an expensive pair of low leather boots came to stand in front of the place where Freddie hid.

"Freddie, we know you're here."

ten

"We're going to cut the crap, Freddie." Agent Kent stared for a moment at the logo on Freddie's polo shirt. "You've been played."

Freddie was holding the map and the USB drives.

"No." Freddie had no idea what Ben had done, but she wasn't going to make it worse. At least, not yet. This *was* Ben, wasn't it? He'd helped her consider this place as "Freddie's" home. It was his plan. She'd listened and he'd explained. It was Ben who'd sent her the SatCar and the map, right? Freddie shook her head. Had she really been so stupid? Life wasn't a *Doctor Who* episode. What wouldn't she believe?

"What do you want, Freddie?" Agent Richards asked.

"What everybody wants," Freddie said. Her chest hurt. This was it. This was the moment when she would lose everything that ever really mattered to her. That's what's asked of women who ask for more. "My family." She stopped. "It sounds silly here and now, but I want to be a good person. I want to love my family." Her voice shook. "But I also want something else. I want to be free."

"Your ego is totally getting in your way."

"Excuse me?" Freddie wasn't expecting any of this—seeing the agents again, hearing "Freddie" in her ear, being trapped in a room deep inside one of The Company (*her husband's*) data centers—but she really wasn't expecting *that*. "My ego?"

"I can neither confirm nor deny anything, but it appears that 'Freddie' wanted to wake you up a little. Perhaps refocus your attention."

"My attention?"

"Everyone wants to be seen," Agent Richards said. "Kind of sweet, actually. Like a Valentine—*here's a break from your everyday disasters*. I think 'Freddie' wanted you to like her. Maybe you got off on the wrong foot."

Freddie didn't want to think about that. "Who is doing this? The Company? Marco?"

"Polo." Agent Richards grinned.

Agent Kent rolled her eyes. "I can neither confirm nor deny . . ."

"Ben?" Freddie was afraid to ask. She *knew* Ben. Didn't she?

Agent Kent held out her hand. "We'll take them now."

Freddie handed over the USB drives, the map, and the badge.

"Mr. Bhattacharya thought of everything." Agent Richards shook his head.

"One memory stick to kill 'Freddie.' And the other to free her. Open source was always what Mr. Bhattacharya wanted. Look, he even has FREE FREDDIE written on the side." Agent Kent held up the green USB drive. "Mr. Bhattacharya made something that is going to change culture. That's the thing about 'Freddie.' You're more likely to be led towards action not apathy."

"Ben built 'Freddie.'" As soon as the words were spoken, Freddie understood that it was something she already knew. *Her first client. Ben knew everyone.* "But then why . . . ?"

"He got hit with a double dose." Agent Richards smiled. "You inspired him perhaps a bit too much. Who knows? Second thoughts?"

"But the plan." Freddie's head ached. "Why would he give me the choice, the power, to bring down everything he'd made? I mean, couldn't he do that for himself?"

"You *are* his Outsourcer," Agent Richards said.

"You didn't help the situation." Agent Kent nodded. "But, then again, he was targeted and primed. Your idealism seemed to have . . . uh . . . rubbed off on him." Both agents looked her in the eye and Freddie kept herself from looking away.

"It was all philosophical until it wasn't." Agent Richards spoke slowly. "It became personal."

"Sometimes we want to break what we build just because we can. But

'Freddie' knew exactly what to do."

"How?" Freddie asked.

"We can neither confirm nor deny," they all said in unison.

"I get it. I guess." Freddie wasn't sure what was what. Who was the enemy? Who were the good guys and girls? She wasn't sure. Mostly, she wasn't sure it even mattered. "I did this," she said instead.

"Can I give you some advice?" Agent Kent sighed. "My forties weren't the struggle that all the media likes to say. The struggle really was coming from inside me. We have phases."

"Well, the moon, obviously," her partner added, his face a mask of complete seriousness. "You don't have to watch much Neil Tyson to get that about all of us, but maybe most of all, women."

"Anyway," Agent Kent snorted. "Freddie, you had your twenties phase, then you had the give-my-family-all-I've-got phase. You're just ending something here."

"This marks a beginning." Agent Richards nodded.

"Who are you really?" Freddie asked. "Are you even real agents?"

"We're exactly who we say we are." Agent Richards smiled.

"The good guys." Agent Kent touched her ear. "Put your earbuds in."

"Why?"

"Just do it."

Freddie put her earbuds in. "Freddie" was *still* talking: "You even suggested cops should sit outside of movie theaters if they really wanted to catch people speeding. You probably don't remember the conversation, but I do . . ."

"She put you in an action movie," Agent Richards whispered. "She gave you what you wanted."

"Don't let it mess with you," Agent Kent said. "Total ego."

Freddie took her earbuds off. "I don't want this." Freddie wasn't certain that was completely truthful. "This used to be fun, but I just want out of here. I want—"

Both agents raised a palm, tilting their heads to show they were listening to someone else. Then, they began talking into their shoulders: "Beta Test Complete. Roger that." Agent Kent moved her hand towards her weapon. "At some point, Freddie, we need to speak further about someone you know." They were leaving.

"What?" Freddie's throat ached.

"You need to get out of this building immediately. Freddie, do not get caught."

"What?" Freddie asked. "Caught by whom?"

"Goodbye, Freddie," Agent Richards called over his shoulder. "Good luck."

Freddie was running faster than before. She tried a door. Locked. The unceasing alarms surrounded her and the red lights flashing above made her dizzy. She pushed her earbuds back in—even "Freddie" would be better than the cacophony of sound—but there was no voice in her head. She kept running. Nothing seemed to open. Doors locked one after another. Lights kept clicking on and off with her motion. She tried to picture where she was as if watching herself on the map.

That's when Freddie saw the exit sign, sans serif, all green lit. She ran hard, praying the door would give way. It did, and she found herself in the hot sun, running over radiating pavement, her eyes burning. Her earphones clicked on, mid-song. "Criminal," of course. *What I need is a good defense*. Freddie pumped her arms.

She ran as hard as she could to the SatCar. The passenger side door was already open. Freddie jumped inside and slammed the door. *Please start! Please!* The screen came on, a picture of poppies in a field beneath a mountain. The wind blowing their red blooms back and forth, and an automated voice: "Take the key."

Freddie was still panting. "Ben?"

Freddie hadn't seen the key before, but there it was in front of her, plugged into the dash. Freddie pulled out the key and the screen flickered. It was the older woman again, the one that looked and sounded a little like Rosemary, but wasn't.

"Freddie . . " The woman was seated, no longer on a stage.

"You're me, aren't you?" Freddie asked, straining to keep her voice steady.

The woman smiled. She did look like Freddie, but she was crisper and infinitely more elegant. Her hair loose and silvery and her clothes the expensive hemp and cashmere get-ups Rosemary always wore. Shoulders on display. Once again, "Freddie" had adapted.

"I'm such a cliché," Freddie said to her virtual elder self. "So derivative."

"So don't be." The woman smiled.

"Ben . . ."

"Ben needs a good attorney. Which he already has. He didn't really need you for all this. He just wanted you to be part of it. Look around you, Freddie. We all have preferences, don't we? We make choices, my dear."

"Shit."

"I just said that to freak you out." The woman laughed. "Freddie, you know who I am. Trust yourself." She paused. "How we behave instructs our future choices, but behavior doesn't have to be completely binary."

"Great time for a lecture." Freddie felt as if she'd been slapped. "Shit! You are me, aren't you?"

"Bingo." The woman nodded. "But I'm better."

"I'm not Rosemary," Freddie said. "I'm not rich. I have responsibilities. I'm nobody. I don't know any—"

The woman smiled and seemed about to say something, but her voice paused and the screen went dark. Freddie was surprised to hear the automated voice again: "Grab the key and get out of this car. Freddie, run as fast as you can. Take the key. Now!"

Which is exactly what Freddie did. And she felt it just as it was about to happen. She turned her head and the force carried her. She fell hard as the bright light reached up into the cloudless sky. There, in the distance. She squinted, her cheek on the concrete. A fire? No—some sort of propeller. The sky. The sun. The desert. The mountains. And above it all, an enormous banner of words: *Wind power! Solar power! And it still isn't enough! This message brought to you by TOTO. Unplug!*

Her earphones miraculously still in, her ears ringing with the faint rhythm of that last interlude of the song. *I need to be redeemed*. It reminded Freddie of the Sunday school songs of her childhood. Of Mrs. Morris chewing gum while playing the stand-up piano, her hair puffed high, shellacked. Freddie's eyes found another source. Too much light. Some sort of Burning Man thing going on. Did it matter anymore what was the truth and what was a lie and what was neither?

Pow, pouf, to the sky. *Don't look up*, Freddie thought. She squinted. A group of people on the other side of the building were carrying banners, pulling solar panels on wheels. Security trucks. People in neon vests. The roof covered in reflective light. They were all on the other side, but the demonstration was beginning to snake around the building.

No one saw her. Not yet. At least, that's what Freddie hoped. *Why am I running?* Freddie thought. No one was chasing her, but they would if they saw her. Maybe if she just stayed low and didn't move. Freddie got closer to the ground and closed her eyes.

And with the last note—that last, long, fluted note—the music stopped, and the voice that began to speak into her ears was no longer "Freddie." It was Pam's voice. And after Pam, Ben, and the rest of Freddie's former clients. Every memoir she'd ever written. First line upon first line, story after story, voice after voice, they spoke the words she'd written for them. Freddie had met them in their homes or in the places they'd felt safe enough to share their lives. She'd seen them and listened. Freddie thought of their faces. The way they had each spoken about pain and love and hurt and joy.

How are we all so brave? Freddie thought.

Maybe for the first time in her life, Freddie stopped. She carried nothing. Freddie pulled out her earbuds and threw them. She lay there in the dirt, the heat of the sun above and the ground below. Sweating, Freddie closed her eyes.

She wanted to stay. Here.

I don't know anything, Freddie thought. But that wasn't true. She knew two things. She knew who she loved and she knew what she loved to do. She needed to tell the truth.

Freddie could hear it coming. When Freddie finally opened her eyes, she saw the car barreling towards her at top speed. She squinted. There was a squeal of tires. Freddie pushed herself up. *A friend is an enemy is a terrorist is a—How can we pick our sides? What if we were chosen? A job, outsourced.*

The car had been coming at her too fast. It screeched into park, and Freddie barely had a chance for recognition when the driver's side door swung open and Mister leapt out.

eleven

Freddie realized she'd been rehearsing the line. Trying it out different ways, the emphasis on various words, until she gave that up as well. Mister gunned their station wagon hard and she reconsidered. *I don't need saved*, she thought. *Saving?*

All the windows were down. Freddie couldn't look at the road or into the mirror. She didn't want to see anything. She didn't care that she hurt, that the motion of the car was the only thing that felt good, somehow. She didn't want to ask. But she did, finally.

"What are you doing here?"

"We had a glitch in the system." He looked over at her. He was screaming over the wind. "A timing issue. I got a call earlier."

"How did you find me?" And then, she realized they were both in the car. Alone. "The kids?"

"I'm not an idiot, Freddie," Mister said. She could barely hear what he was saying. Her ears were ringing. She watched his lips. "They're with Mirabel. Not that it's important right now, but that new nursing home job is messing with her hours already. She couldn't work yesterday. She needs your help with it. So she asked if she could come today." Freddie stared at him. "And then, I got the call to come here." He stopped, his voice thick. "And you were here."

"I never said . . ." Freddie began, her head still ringing. "But how?"

He pointed to her phone. His fingers briefly touched her wrist.

"The same way I know that you're coming home from the grocery store so we can have the garage door open. The same way that I know you're safe walking around the neighborhood at night. The same way I know when you're coming back from a run." He stopped and swallowed hard. "You don't get it. You still don't get it. Maybe you never have."

"What?" There was gravel in the side of her cheek. Her khakis were torn, and she could see her skin beneath, bloody and bare. Her left arm where she'd landed was a mess. None of it mattered. "What? Tell me. I want to know. What?"

He picked up his phone from the dashboard and tossed it on her lap. She flinched.

"I don't know your code." It sounded both pathetic and mean. *Your password. Your digits. Your secrets aren't safe, even with me.*

"Here!" *Still! Still he didn't give her his code.* He pressed it in himself. "There."

And there was the map. And the red pin.

"You!" Mister screamed. "You are my map."

There was nothing to answer. No choice to be made yet. No ending in sight. Everything bad and good. And, maybe for the first time, in this moment, no place else she would rather be.

He looked over at her. "Aren't you going to say something? Anything?"

They sat in their seats. No music, just the wind.

"Do I even want to know?" he asked, eyes on the key she held.

"It's nothing," she answered, her thumb in the indentations. It was shaped like a diamond, one angle pointing up and the other pointing down. It was the space in between where you could hold. "That's a lie. I want to tell you. I want you to tell me. I want us to—" *We all have our maps*, Freddie thought. *What we know and what we don't. So much certainty!* "I don't even know," she answered.

"I've never seen one in real life. *Project Roof.*" He stared at her. "Freddie?"

She threw the key out the window. "I've never done that before," she yelled. She'd just littered.

"It'll just come back to you," he said. "It's the new prototype at work. They invented a house key that can never be lost."

116

Freddie thought of many things in that minute. Her children. This man she'd built her life around. A fragment of that speech on the screen in the SatCar when she was salvia'd: "It's the people in the home that will change this world, but only if we take that step out the door. Towards our neighbor, towards our friend, towards our enemy—this is the true social network. Both words and deeds; we must learn better how to help each other."

Sure, there was that, but there was also this. *You understand I'm probably going to lose my job*. He hadn't said it yet, but he would. He would ask if that is what she'd wanted all along. And maybe she would answer if she knew.

"You act like I don't know you," he said, staring at the road.

"I'm not sure you do," Freddie answered.

"The same goes for me," he said. "Did you ever think about that?"

She almost didn't hear it over the wind. It took her a minute.

"Do you know *me*?" he asked. "Don't you ever think I'd like something else sometimes? We used to have fun."

James, this man she'd married, this man beside her, in profile—he was here. And then he turned towards her. James. A real person. This was his life too.

"Do you even want to know me?" he asked. It hurt her to see his face. *I never wanted to hurt you*, she thought. *I have never lied to you. I never will.*

"Yes," she answered. "I do. I want to."

"Do you love me? Not just us, not just our family. Listen to me, Freddie. Do you love *me*?"

"Yes." It felt like she was choking. "I forgot for a minute. I made you the enemy."

"You did," he said. And that's when she saw it. Admittedly, she was trying hard to see it, to see anything. And he was trying just as hard, but there it was.

"Can't we start over from here?" she asked. "In this place, where we both are right now." She looked out the window. "Wherever we are. Can we?"

And that's when he said it.

epilogue

Freddie went in again to cover her children. The boy sleeping. The girl awake, writing out math problems on pink construction paper. Freddie covered her girl again.

"I'm glad you're home."

"Me too."

"Just a minute. Four, three, two." The girl finished her problem. She set her work down. Capped her marker. "Tell me a story," the girl said. Thumb to mouth, blankie in hand. She usually said: *Tell me a story of when you were a girl. Start at the beginning. Don't stop till the end.*

"Tell me yours?" Freddie asked. She looked at that face.

"Someday," her daughter answered. "Not today."

And so Freddie began. *This is what a girl did.*

Acknowledgments

October 2017, Northern California

I wrote this book six years ago while living in Mountain View, California. I picked it back up three years ago to revise during a wet winter in the South of England. It found its way to Minerva Rising Press while I was living in Austin, Texas. And now, I am writing my acknowledgements in the last place I ever expected—back in Northern California. The Universe has a mighty fine sense of humor.

There are so many people in all of those places we have lived that I would like to thank—friends who offered comfort, beverages, daily life assistance, a smile, or even simply their forgiveness when I was grumpy or staring off into space. Having a friend who writes is a mixed bag of tricks. Thank you, my friends.

This is such a special opportunity to thank my NorCal friends in particular—the OG crew who have loved me and my family through thick and thin. NorCal is beautiful, but you, dear friends, are the best part.

This opportunity to thank mentors I have had along the way, as well as the writing community in Indianapolis, Indiana, and the wonderful MFA program I am grateful to have attended at Butler University, is one I don't take lightly. I am very proud to be an Indiana writer, even if my travels have taken me elsewhere. Susan Neville, Barbara Shoup, James Watt, Dan Barden, Andy Levy, Michael Dahlie, Dianne Martin, Hilene Flanzbaum, Lili Wright, and all the other amazing teachers I've been lucky enough to learn from, I owe you such a debt of gratitude. Thank you also to my fantastic community of Indiana writer friends and especially to my first writer friend, the incredible Bryan Furuness, for inspiring me these past decades.

Thank you to all at Minerva Rising Press for your dedication and thoughtfulness.

If being a friend to a writer is challenging at times, imagine being a parent, partner, or child of one. Mixed bag is an understatement. To my parents, thank you, THANK YOU. To my husband and children, you are my heart.

Most of all, I want to acknowledge you. You—the woman writing while others sleep. Take heart. Keep writing.

Author Biography

Eliza Tudor's stories have appeared in *Hobart*, *PANK*, *Annalemma*, *Paper Darts*, and elsewhere, including the anthology *Mythic Indy*. She recently returned to Northern California, where she lives with her family.

Photo by Mona Gohil